"Danny has a big day tomorrow. He has to go to the hospital," Lizzie reminded their daughter.

"But we're going with him," Emma said. "Just like you always take me when I have tests, Mommy."

"Thank you," Danny said, eyeing Lizzie's hesitant expression. "I am a little nervous."

"Don't you worry," said Emma. "We'll be right there with you. If you like, you can hold my hand. It makes it better when someone holds your hand."

Such a solemn offering, it made Lizzie want to cry. Emma had been through too much at her age, and it broke her heart to see how deeply her daughter could understand the potential for pain in someone else—but it also made her proud. Holding back her emotions, she gave her daughter a kiss and slipped from the bed. "Sleep well, Emma."

"You too, Mom." She reached for Danny for a kiss, as well.

He only hesitated for a second before he gave her a long hug and a quick peck on the forehead. "I'm..." He cleared his throat. "I'm so happy to know you, Emma."

Her eyes glinted. "I'm glad you're my dad. And I am so happy you are here to help me, too."

And with that, she rendered him speechless.

* * *

THE STIRLING RANCH:
Where home—and love—await you...

Dear Reader,

I can't tell you how excited I am about this story, my first book for Harlequin Special Edition. Not just because I fell in love with the characters and want to jump into their world, but because writing a book for Harlequin has been a long-held dream of mine. I have to say, when I picked up my first Harlequin novel, I never would have dreamed that I would one day actually write one. All I knew was that I wanted more, more, more! Fortunately, I could have more.

It was summer in Stuttgart (where my father was stationed while I was in college) and we had one English TV station (American Forces Radio and Television Service—AFRTS). I had time on my hands and little to do, so I turned to the Harlequin bookshelf at the base library. I'd borrow three books on one day and return them for three more on the next. When I ran out of books, which I eventually did, I played at writing my own. This led to a decades-long affair with romance and writing.

When I was finally published in 2011, I was thrilled and humbled that people actually loved *my* books as much as I had loved others' books. How delicious is it that now, on the tenth anniversary of my first release, my very first Harlequin story is being published?

I hope you enjoy your visit to Butterscotch Ridge with Danny, Lizzie, Emma and the whole Stirling family. I'd love to hear your thoughts! Check out all my books and contests on sabrinayork.com, and if you want to get updates about future books and tiara giveaways—and snag a free book—sign up for my newsletter at sabrinayork.com/gift.

Happy reading, my darlings!

Sabrina York

Accidental Homecoming

—

SABRINA YORK

H HARLEQUIN

SPECIAL
EDITION

HARLEQUIN®
SPECIAL
EDITION™

Recycling programs
for this product may
not exist in your area.

ISBN-13: 978-1-335-40802-0

Accidental Homecoming

Harlequin Enterprises ULC
22 Adelaide St. West, 40th Floor
Toronto, Ontario M5H 4E3, Canada
www.Harlequin.com

Printed in U.S.A.

Sabrina York is the *New York Times* and *USA TODAY* bestselling author of hot, humorous romance. She loves to explore contemporary, historical and paranormal genres, and her books range from sweet and sexy to scorching romance. Her awards include the 2018 HOLT Medallion and the National Excellence in Romantic Fiction Award, and she was also a 2017 RITA® Award nominee for Historical Romance. She lives in the Pacific Northwest with her husband of thirty-plus years and a very drooly Rottweiler.

Visit her website at sabrinayork.com to check out her books, excerpts and contests.

Books by Sabrina York

Harlequin Special Edition

The Stirling Ranch
Accidental Homecoming

Visit the Author Profile page
at Harlequin.com for more titles.

To Susan Litman for extraordinary patience
and for making this dream come true.

Chapter One

Of all the reckless things Danny Diem had done in his life, this was by far the most reckless—driving nine hundred miles to the middle of nowhere based on a scrap of a letter, a whisper of hope. But when a guy was as desperate as he was, sometimes reckless was the only option.

Now, here he was, smack-dab in the middle of the most alien landscape he'd ever experienced. And for a guy born and raised in Las Vegas that was saying a lot.

Everywhere he looked—left, right, forward, back—there was nothing. Rolling hills of hay-colored grasses as far as the eye could see. No structures. No towns. No living creatures. Just…

emptiness. The cloudless sky arched overhead in what seemed like an endless bowl of blue.

It would have been pretty, he supposed, if wide-open spaces didn't make him a little twitchy. He was used to the thrum of the city, the glare of neon lights and street noise. Police sirens, boisterous crowds, all-night bacchanals...

There was no noise out here, other than the whistling of the wind.

It was downright eerie.

The only thing that felt familiar to him was the sweltering early September heat as summer refused to quit.

His GPS told him he was only twenty miles or so from his destination, but he had the sneaking suspicion it was lying. That he would never reach civilization again. That he'd be driving through this barren countryside forever. Hopefully, this whole scenario wasn't God's way of making a joke.

Hot air blew in through his open windows as he zoomed down the deserted two-lane highway that, in parts, didn't even bother with lane markers. Sweat dripped down the back of his neck and trickled between his shoulder blades. The sun baked the exposed side of his face. He reached for his water bottle and then grimaced as he realized it was empty. He resisted the urge to try the air-conditioning again, because he knew damn well it had conked out somewhere in Idaho.

He'd been foolishly optimistic to think his old

'Vette could make the long trip from Vegas unscathed. But then, when you had few options, it was easy to convince yourself that optimism was realistic. And the letter he'd received had seemed like a lifeline. One he'd never expected. One that made this trip a gamble he couldn't afford to pass up.

He glanced at the official-looking document on the passenger seat under his duffle bag, the edges riffling in the wind, and once again, his thoughts returned to his father. That big, looming shadow in his life.

Whoever he'd been, he hadn't wanted anything to do with his son, or the woman who had produced him. Strange that now, at the lowest point in Danny's life, this man might actually come to his rescue.

No one had ever come to Danny's rescue before. Other than an on-again, off-again mother and one far-too-short love affair, he'd always been utterly on his own. It had always been up to him to find a way, any way, to wriggle out of his problems. This time, it seemed there was no way out.

And then the letter had come.

As legal documents went, it was frustratingly vague. All it said was that Danny was included in the will of a man named Daniel Stirling I, and he was to present himself at the offices of William Watney, Esquire, in the town of Butterscotch Ridge in eastern Washington State. It didn't specify how much the inheritance was, or why Danny was included. He could only imagine that the deceased was his deadbeat father, the man his mother had cursed since Danny was small. But even that was conjecture. Hell, everything to do with that part of his past was conjecture, considering he knew practically nothing about the man.

Well, hell. In all likelihood, his inheritance was something useless. Like a grandfather clock or a packet of old love letters. This whole thing was probably a waste of time, but in his dire straits, it was a necessary one.

His life could hardly get any worse. Could it?

A huge *ker-chunk* shook his car and a plume of steam roiled up from under the hood. The car sputtered and jerked, then slowly rolled to a stop on the side of the road.

Damn. Maybe I shouldn't have asked.

He sighed and reached down to pop the hood, which let out a great gasp of vapor. Awesome. He checked his cell phone, but as he expected, out here there was no reception. He was stranded. In the middle of nowhere, in a hellish summer heat wave.

Great. Another disaster. He seemed doomed to find them.

Danny hadn't seen another car since he'd left the Tri-Cities, and while he'd spotted a solar-powered call box, he couldn't say how many miles back it had been. He had no idea how far it was to the next town. Too far to walk with no water, for sure.

The car was fast becoming too hot to sit in, as

it soaked up the blistering sunshine, so Danny grabbed his baseball cap, which he hoped would protect him from the heat, propped open the hood in the hopes the engine would cool, then settled down in a slender shady spot on the far side of the car and prayed for someone to come along.

If he had to, he'd wait until nightfall and then start the long walk to civilization—a gas station, a far-flung country motel, something. Hopefully it would be cooler by then.

As he settled down to wait, one thought buzzed through his brain. Where on earth had he gotten the idea that Washington State was cold and rainy?

He must have dozed off, because he woke with a start from a familiar dream when he heard the roar of an approaching engine. The dream was alluring—it was the one he had often, where he and Lizzie were together in each other's arms. *His lips sliding over her skin, tasting her. Her scent engulfing him. The sound of her moan in his ears so vivid it seemed she was right there beside him...* The dream came to him so often and felt so real that it was hard to shake. It still clung to him as he leaped to his feet and frantically waved his arms.

An enormous crew cab slowed and pulled to the shoulder in front of Danny's Corvette, and the driver stepped out. His boots were dusty and well-worn, but it was the Stetson that made clear, beyond a shadow of a doubt, that Danny had landed in cowboy country.

The man was about his age, maybe a few years older. His face was weathered and his chin sported an auburn bristle. His eyes were gray and he had a friendly smile.

"Hey there, fella. You need some help?" he asked in a deep, smoker's rasp.

"Yeah. If you don't mind." Danny gestured at his sad little car. "Engine conked out."

The cowboy sauntered over and gave the 'Vette's engine a quick glance. "Probably the heat. Did you try adding coolant to the radiator?"

"Uh, I don't have any."

"Water, then?"

A rush of heat rose on Danny's face. He'd never felt more stupid. "I'm out of water." He'd brought plenty—he'd thought—but apparently not enough. He hadn't realized he'd be traveling through this searing terrain. In *rainy* Washington State. In September.

The cowboy didn't smirk or make a rude comment about city boys. He just nodded, tipped back his hat with a finger and said, "Well, let's have a look."

He bent over the engine and fiddled with this or that—Danny had no idea, because, honestly, he knew little to nothing about mechanical things—and then the fellow grunted. "Well, water won't help. Looks like your whole radiator's blown. You're gonna need a tow. Can I give you a ride to town?"

Danny blew out a sigh of relief, took off his cap

and wiped the sweat from his brow. "That would be great." He turned to the cowboy with a grin, only to discover that the guy was staring at him.

As soon as he realized that Danny had noticed his sharp attention, he averted his gaze. "I'm Chase McGruder, by the way," he said, thrusting out his hand.

"Danny. Danny Diem."

Chase narrowed his eyes. "Have we met?"

"Ever been to Vegas?"

The response was a snort.

"Then, no. I don't think so."

Chase peered at him for a few more seconds and then shook his head. "Huh. You look familiar, but I just can't place it. Ah, it'll come to me. Well, we better get movin'. Need to get you out of this heat, I reckon." He paused and pointed back to Danny's car. "You may want to bring your things, though. George has the only shop in town, and he tends to start drinking early on the weekends, so he may not get out here for a while."

Danny chuckled. "Ah…it's Thursday."

Chase's grin was wry. "Exactly."

Danny nodded and headed back to grab the letter and his duffel bag. Everything he owned was in that duffle. So pathetic. But that was what happened, he supposed, when your dear, sweet mother cleaned out your bank account, then cleaned out your apartment and pawned anything of value before disappearing into the wind.

He could have used those resources—any resources—about now. He was in debt to Mikey Gerardo, Vegas's roughest loan shark, with interest mounting and another payment looming—all thanks to dear old Mom.

Thrusting all those dark thoughts from his mind, he hooked the bag over his shoulder and followed Chase to the crew cab. He had to wait while his new buddy cleared the passenger seat of empty juice boxes and toys, tossing them into the back. He shot Danny a wry grin. "You have kids?"

"Nope," he said. All throughout his life, that was a message his mother had pounded into his brain. *Children ruin your life.* He'd certainly ruined hers. She'd made that more than clear. Naturally, he'd long ago vowed to avoid such a disaster. But then, he thought with a bitter twist in his gut, he'd managed to ruin his life all on his own. With a sigh, he hoisted himself up onto the step and into the truck.

"Married?" Chase asked as Danny joined him in the cab.

"Nope." He had no idea why Lizzie sprang to mind just then—he had no idea why he still bothered to think about her anymore—but when Chase turned over the engine and the air-conditioning kicked on, he let all thoughts of her waft away in a frigid blast.

"Well, be warned. As soon as you're married, your truck'll never be your own again." Chase chuckled, reached into a cooler behind the seat and handed Danny a cold bottle of water.

He grabbed it with gusto. Damn. Plain old water had never looked so good. He downed the bottle in two gulps, which made Chase chuckle again and hand him another. It occurred to Danny that Chase was a pretty happy guy, judging by how often he chuckled. But why wouldn't he be happy? He had air-conditioning and a cooler filled with water bottles.

"Thanks," Danny said after he took a deep draw of the second bottle. "For the water. And the ride."

"No problem." Chase set the truck in gear and headed down the lonely road. "We don't get a lot of visitors in Butterscotch Ridge."

Danny gave him the side-eye. "How do you know I'm going to Butterscotch Ridge?"

Chase shrugged. "Few folks take this road to go anywhere else. BR is a real small town. Small enough, I s'pose, that the locals figure it doesn't even deserve all those syllables."

Danny aimed the AC vent to blow directly on his face. "How does a town get a name like Butterscotch Ridge, anyway?" He didn't care, but he figured he owed this guy conversation at least.

"Easy." Chase shot him a wink. "The town founder's wife thought the grasses looked like butterscotch in the dry season."

Danny glanced out the window at the passing

range—which was, in a word, brown—and shook his head. Whatever worked, he supposed.

"So what's the town like?" he asked.

Chase shrugged. "Nice. Quiet. Though it can get rowdy at my place on a Saturday night." He waggled his eyebrows. "See, I own the only bar in town."

Danny huffed a laugh. "Pretty sure we'll meet again, then."

"Yup. In a town like this, gossip is better than gold. On that note…why are you here, anyway?"

Danny turned back to the window. Watched butterscotch-colored weeds flick by. "Need to meet with William Watney." What else was there to say? He didn't know much else.

"Bill? You in some kinda trouble?"

"No." He hoped not. "It's a legal matter. I'll get more details when I see him."

"Yeah. Bill can be vague. But he's a good lawyer. I'm sure he'll take good care of you, whatever it is."

"Yeah."

They rode for a while in silence and then they passed an enormous gate that made Danny's heart hiccup. The wood-burned sign swinging above read Stirling Ranch. Seeing the name from the letter made something in his belly curl. "Hey," he said as casually as he could. "What's that place?"

Chase grunted. "That's where the Stirling family lives. Local royalty. Family's been here forever. They own a successful beef ranch. In fact, they own about half of the town, too."

A strange feeling needled Danny. It was all he could do to stay focused on the conversation. He jokingly asked, "Who owns the other half?"

Chase didn't seem amused. His lip curled. "The Cages." He glanced at Danny. "Just a heads-up, by the way. There's a huge feud between the Stirlings and the Cages."

"A feud? Over what?" *And who are the Cages? What kind of town is this, anyway?*

Chase barked a laugh. "Who the hell even remembers? But it's been going on for decades."

"Good to know." Danny filed away that tidbit and stared out of the window as this all percolated in his brain. Especially the *successful-ranch* part. Though he had no idea what to expect, no idea what the will actually said. With any luck, he might inherit enough money to pay off his debts and maybe have a little left over to start up life somewhere else. Somewhere far from Vegas. The idea gave him hope. Something he wasn't used to feeling. Naturally, he didn't trust it.

He sat up a little straighter as he caught a glimpse of a town on the horizon. It grew as they approached, the image of it waffling in the heat, making it seem like a mirage. As they drove down the main street, Danny caught sight of neatly painted storefronts and a town green with an actual gazebo. Just what you'd think a small town would be like. Where everybody knew your name and folks looked out for each other.

Yeah. A mirage.

Chase pulled up in front of a rather grand facade with *William Watney, Esquire*, emblazoned on the shingle. He snorted, pointing to a sign hanging on the doorknob. Watney had apparently *Gone Fishin'*.

"Looks like Bill's off the clock," Chase said, backing out of the spot. "Where are you staying?"

Danny blinked. Where was he staying? He had some cash, but not a lot. He'd been planning to sleep in his car, as he had on the way here, to save money. Obviously, that plan was shot. "I… Is there a hotel?"

"Sure. The Butterscotch Inn. Just down the road."

"Awesome."

"Listen, I'll drop you there so you can check in, then come on by the B&G—" he pointed to a rambling, large-windowed establishment, which proclaimed it had the best steak in the Columbia Valley, as they passed "—and I'll buy you dinner."

"You don't need to do that." The guy had already helped him immensely. He hated to take advantage.

"I know." Chase winked. "Let's call it a down payment on the scoop you're gonna give me once you talk to Bill."

That sounded like a plan. Besides, Danny's belly was starting to grumble. Still, after Chase dropped him off at the hotel, and he checked into his— *air-conditioned!*—room, Danny flopped down on the bed. He needed a moment or two to reflect on everything he'd learned. And everything he hadn't.

Of course, he ended up thinking mostly about Lizzie. He always did. Even though it was water under a very old bridge.

Even now, more than five years later, he wished he could go back and change things. Wished he hadn't said or done whatever had made her realize he wasn't the man she'd needed him to be. He could only imagine that she'd decided she deserved someone better. Someone less...broken. His mother had told him he didn't deserve Lizzie. Apparently, she'd been right.

If only Lizzie hadn't changed her cell number. If only he knew where she was, and that she was safe and whole.

But mostly, he wished she was here. That he could talk to her about all this. He missed talking to her. Mostly, he missed having someone he could trust in his life.

With a grimace, he reminded himself harshly that he couldn't trust her. Couldn't depend on her.

After all, she'd up and left him. Just like everyone else in his life had done.

Granted, they'd been fighting, but they'd fought before—mostly about his mother, or Darla—and Lizzie had stayed by his side. What had been different about *that* fight that had driven her away? He'd asked himself that question a thousand times and never found an answer.

It was a damn shame he couldn't ask her, because

after that night, she'd disappeared, and he'd never been able to track her down.

Yep. Somehow, he'd blown the best thing that ever happened to him. What he wouldn't give to have a chance—any chance—to win her back.

Elizabeth Michaels toyed with her necklace as she stared out of the windows of Seattle Children's Hospital. She barely noticed the bright and shiny day, or the hint of Lake Washington in the distance, or the snow-capped mountains on the horizon.

When she realized what she was doing, she let the necklace fall. Emma had noticed she fiddled with it when she was worried, and she didn't want to let on.

Emma noticed everything.

Lizzie glanced back at the bed, where her daughter was solving a maze in a puzzle book one of the nurses had brought by. She'd always been a curious child, and clever beyond her years. Not satisfied to simply color, she needed more of a challenge.

Well, life had certainly given her a challenge. One she might not survive this time. This time, her weakened immune system didn't seem to be responding to treatment.

As emotion bubbled up in Lizzie's throat, she turned back to the window.

"What is it, Mommy?" Emma asked, her voice slightly muffled through her Minnie Mouse mask.

"Nothing, hon. I just thought I saw an eagle. But wouldn't you know? It was just another seagull."

Emma's tinkle of a laugh made her smile. Made tears prick at Lizzie's eyes. "Mommy, we're in the city. Eagles don't like the city."

"Don't they?" She pinned a smile on her face and moved across the room to plop on the bed. "Who told you that?"

"Everyone knows that." Emma's eyes crinkled above the mask, so Lizzie knew she was grinning.

"I think we should ask Dr. Blake. He would know."

"Mmm. Dr. Blake." Emma's eyebrows did a tango. "He's cute."

"Yes. He's very cute." Also very young. Like, way young. "Maybe you can date him when you get older."

Emma dissolved into giggles and fell back on her pillow. "He's too old for me."

"Is he?"

"Yeah. I thought he would be cute for you, Mommy."

"For me?" Egads. The thought was a little frightening. Lizzie had been single for so long, she didn't even think she would remember how things worked.

Well, she probably would remember, but it hardly mattered. She had too much on her plate to even consider romance with her daughter's doctor, or anyone. Not only was Emma's illness complicated and deadly, it was also expensive. This stay alone would cost thousands. As a contract employee for a local accounting firm, all insurance and most medical costs were out of pocket. *Her* pocket.

Lizzie thrust her financial apprehensions out of her head and focused on her daughter. Nothing was more important than Emma. She would do whatever it took to make her well again.

"Ms. Michaels?"

She bolted off the bed and whirled around as Dr. Blake entered the room. And, yes, he was handsome. Tall and dark-haired, with sculpted features. But he was a baby. Practically. "Dr. Blake. Perhaps you can solve a riddle for us?" she said.

He leaned down and ruffled Emma's hair. "I'd be happy to."

"It's about eagles," Emma said.

"Hmm. Not my area of expertise, but shoot."

"Do they live in the city?"

He grinned down at Lizzie's daughter. "Indeed they do." Emma groaned, and he added, "I saw one in a video from the Woodland Park Zoo just the other day."

"Zoos don't count!" Emma insisted.

"Don't they?" Dr. Dreamboat winked at Lizzie. "I think they do."

"Oh, brother," Emma huffed, and went back to her maze.

The second the child looked away, the doctor's expression sobered. "Ms. Michaels, can I speak to you for a moment?"

Lizzie's belly plummeted. Those were not words

a parent wanted to hear at Children's Hospital. Not after a week like this. "Um, sure. Emma, honey, Dr. Blake and I are going to have a chat. You know where your button is if you need anything, right?"

"Mmm-hmm." She was too engrossed in her maze to even look up.

Dr. Blake took her arm—another bad sign—and Lizzie swallowed heavily. He led her down the sunnily painted hall to a consult room, which was also done up in incongruous cheer. He shot her a conciliatory glance as he waved at a chair.

And she knew.

"It's not working," she said. Might as well face it outright.

He eased a box of tissues toward her and she took one, just in case. "It's not. I'm sorry. We had hoped the bone-marrow stimulants would take before the immunosuppressants began undermining her immune system."

Lizzie sighed and mangled her tissue. She knew what that meant. Only one option left. "So we need to look for a donor."

"Yes. I see she doesn't have any siblings, which are our first choice in these cases. How about close family?"

Lizzie shook her head. "I have a sister, but the minute Emma was diagnosed, we both got tested. Neither of us are compatible." It was hard to keep her voice from cracking under the enormous weight of such simple words.

Dr. Blake set his hand on hers and squeezed. "Related donors are best, but don't worry. There are a lot of success stories with unrelated donors. And Emma is a strong girl. She's a fighter."

How Lizzie hated those words. They were true, but why should a five-year-old have to fight at all? Why should she have to fight for her life?

"What about...?" The doctor cleared his throat. "On the father's side?"

Lizzie's chin came up so fast she bit her tongue. "I beg your pardon?"

"Emma's father? Would he be willing to—?"

"No." He wouldn't be willing to...anything.

"Is there a chance? If he or his family are matches—"

"He doesn't have any family." Just a heartless mother. "Besides, I don't even know where he is." She hadn't seen him since—since that awful fight. What was it? Five and a half years ago?

Dr. Blake nodded. "All right. I just thought I'd bring it up. We'll go ahead and start the process of searching for donors. I'm not going to sugarcoat this, Ms. Michaels." She wished he'd stop calling her that. "But with Emma's blood type, it may take some time to find a good match. You do understand what that means."

She did. A chill racked her. Everything else had failed. Emma had only one slim hope left: finding a compatible donor with an extremely rare blood type.

They both stood, but as Lizzie turned to leave the

room, the doctor sighed and scrubbed at his face. "I just want you to know, Ms. Michaels, everyone here is determined to do our best for your daughter. We care deeply about Emma, too." When his voice broke, it nearly broke her.

"I know, Doctor." She patted his hand. The irony that she was comforting *him* was not lost on her.

She watched him head back to the nurses' station with a heavy heart, confronted with the harsh reality that she'd been able to hold back for months. This time, Emma might not win.

The facts were plain and simple. Emma needed a marrow donor. Blood relatives were the best options. She had no choice other than to track down Danny Diem—and fast—and ask for his help to save their daughter. Which was complicated, because he had no idea he had a daughter. He had no idea that he was a father at all.

Chapter Two

Lizzie's gut roiled.

The thought of telling Danny about Emma terrified her. He'd been pretty clear how he felt about any kind of commitment, the last time they'd talked—although *talked* was hardly the word for it.

She probably should have just told him about the pregnancy then, but she hadn't wanted him to feel obligated to be with her because of the baby. She'd *never* expected his discouraging response when she broached the subject of marriage and children. *I will never get married*, he'd said. *I will never have children*, he'd said. It had broken her heart. Because she knew it meant they couldn't stay together.

She'd packed up and left the next day, never to look back.

And now, it seemed, she needed him.

Or Emma did. Emma needed him desperately.

There was no running from that.

So she would find Danny Diem and ask him to be tested to see if he was a viable donor. And she'd be damned if anything was going to stop her.

Except…finding Danny was harder than she expected.

The first thing she did was call his cell phone, but the woman who answered made it clear there was no Danny at that number. Then Lizzie went to Facebook and Google and even LinkedIn in an attempt to track him down online, but that failed, as well.

How aggravating! Who wasn't on social media?

She spent the rest of the day calling all their mutual friends in Vegas, but none of them had seen Danny for ages. It was as though he'd dropped off the planet. Or dropped all his old friends.

His mother, apparently, had skipped bail on a petty theft charge and disappeared, so there was no help there, and Danny's landlord said his apartment had been cleaned out.

Finally, realizing she had no other options, she called Darla.

Darla Wheeler was last on her list for a reason. The woman had been in love with Danny for years, and while she wasn't the reason he and Lizzie had broken up, her constant plots and ploys to lure him away hadn't helped. Frankly, making nice through an entire conversation with Darla—for the sole benefit of one's child—should be grounds for sainthood.

It annoyed her to no end that Darla, of all people, had the scoop on Danny's whereabouts. After a long, circuitous conversation, she finally revealed that the scuttlebutt was that Danny had left Vegas for a town called Butterscotch Ridge because he'd been named in someone's will.

Lizzie had no idea who might be inclined to leave Danny anything—since his only known relative was his mother, who wouldn't share a stick of gum—and she had no clue where Butterscotch Ridge might be. It took a quick internet search to discover it was in eastern Washington, just over the mountains. Just a five-hour drive from Seattle.

Something about his proximity lifted her soul and, for the first time since Dr. Blake's pronouncement, she felt a whisper of hope.

Darla didn't have Danny's cell number—or wouldn't give it to her—so Lizzie decided to go to this town and try to find him. She couldn't take Emma, of course. It was too risky, not knowing what lay ahead. She would not expose her daughter to rejection, if that was the way it went. Aside from that, Emma needed a sterile environment. Hotels and ranches were notoriously germy. She couldn't take even the smallest chance of Emma picking up a bug. Not with her immune system so vulnerable.

As it happened, the doctors decided to extend Emma's hospital stay over the weekend. Oh, they'd assured Lizzie that everything looked fine—they just wanted to observe her and run a few tests—but over the past six months, Lizzie had become super sensitized to hidden messages. She couldn't help but think that time was running out.

She needed to find Danny and talk to him, *now*.

It only made sense that she leave for Butterscotch Ridge right away.

"I don't like the idea," Nan said bluntly.

Lizzie sighed as she pulled her suitcase out of the closet and dropped it on the bed. "What don't you like?"

Her sister shook her head. "All of it. I mean, you're heading off to track down the ex who broke your heart. Do you remember how you were when you got here? Because I do. That guy crushed you. People don't change."

"Emma needs him."

"There's no guarantee he's a match." Nan caught Lizzie's expression and sighed. "Look, it's your life. Your daughter. Your heart. Do what you need to do. I'm behind you no matter what. Just be careful."

"Thank you." Lizzie hugged her sister. "That's exactly what I needed right now. Oh. That, and someone to stay with Emma at the hospital."

Nan grinned. "You know I will." She was as much a mom to Emma as Lizzie. "Be sure you keep me posted while you're gone."

"Of course."

"My phone is always on for you."

"I know."

Nan was quiet for a second, then she said, "She'll be all right, you know? It'll only be for a few days."

"I know she will."

Nan sat on the bed next to the open suitcase and gusted a sigh. "Of course, it's not *us* I'm worried about."

"Me? I'll be fine." She would. No matter what. And she refused to let any lurking fear claim her.

"It's a long drive to eastern Washington."

"Only five hours or so." Lizzie stared at the outfits she'd laid out on the bed. She didn't know why she couldn't decide what to take. It wasn't as though she needed to impress Danny. She was going to see him for one reason only. Emma.

It still made her mind spin to know Danny was so close. She totally ignored any emotions other than relief. Shoved them back into the dark box that had held them for so long. Emotions were a luxury she couldn't afford. And thinking about Danny— about their troubled past—was pointless.

Nan flopped back on the pillows, her bottle-blond hair splaying in dramatic fashion. "What on earth is he doing in some tiny cow town, of all places?"

Lizzie shrugged and picked the dress with red cherries, rolled it up and placed it in her suitcase. She'd always loved that dress. "Darla said something about an inheritance."

Nan's brow wrinkled. "I thought he didn't have family…other than that horrible mother of his."

"Now, now." Lizzie forced a smile, though it wasn't funny. Danny's mother had done everything she could to break them up, way back when. For no reason whatsoever, she shoved her little black dress into her bag, too. Just in case something came up. Not that it would.

She closed her suitcase and sat next to her sister with a sigh. Nan slipped her arm around Lizzie's shoulder and gave it a squeeze. "It's going to be all right," she said, though they both knew the outcome was far from certain. Because Lizzie was headed out to confront the man she'd once loved. The man who hadn't loved her enough to want more.

How would he react when she told him he was a father? The question kept her tossing and turning all night.

In the morning, she put her suitcase into the trunk of her car and went to the hospital with Nan at her side. As she walked into Emma's room, she put on a bright smile, though it cost her.

She'd never left Emma. Never. Not even for a day. Certainly not for an entire weekend. The fact that her baby was still in the hospital battling an infection didn't help at all.

"Hello, pumpkin. How are you doing this morning?" She kissed her daughter in greeting.

Emma's eyes crinkled over her mask. "There were pancakes for breakfast."

"Ooh," Nan cooed. "Lucky you." Pancakes were Emma's favorite.

"With blueberries."

"Blueberries?" Lizzie widened her eyes. "Wow."

"Classy stuff," Nan said as she sat by Emma on the bed.

The child's eyes went solemn. "Blueberries have antioxi ants."

"Antioxidants?" Nan, a lawyer, liked to clarify every fact.

Emma nodded. "They're good for me."

"Taste good, too," Lizzie said with a forced smile. "Listen, hon, I have to…" Heavens, this was hard to say.

Nan hopped in to help. "Your mom's going on a little business trip."

Emma's expression clouded. "What?"

Lizzie glared at Nan. She could have broken it more gently. "It's only for a few days. I'll be back before you're even ready to come home. Aunt Nan's going to stay with you. Is that okay?"

Emma swallowed. "Only for a few days?"

Lizzie hated that her little mask trembled. "I promise."

"We'll do some fun things," Nan assured her.

"They said I can bring in some DVDs. We can watch *The Lion King* again."

Soulful brown eyes brightened. "I love that movie. Can we have ice cream, too?"

Nan blinked. She glanced at Lizzie for guidance.

"You know you need to ask the nurses," she told her daughter. "But I'm sure some special treats can be arranged."

"Well, all right, then."

It was a trifle discomfiting that Emma accepted these concessions so easily. It was, after all, the first time they'd ever been apart. In her entire life. Lizzie had expected a tear at least. It took a moment for her to swallow an inappropriate sense of umbrage. It was a good thing, after all, that Emma didn't need to rely on her alone. Wasn't it?

"You'd better get going," Nan said.

Lizzie frowned at her. "Trying to get rid of me?"

"You have a long drive."

She sighed. "I suppose." Loath to leave, she jangled her car keys and then, at Nan's glance, bent down to hug her daughter. "You be good, all right?"

"I'm always good," Emma responded.

"I'll be good, too," Nan said with a wink, snuggling into the bed at Emma's side.

"Did you bring the movie with you?" Emma asked, that easily sloughing off her mother's clinging angst.

"I most certainly did." Nan produced it from her

purse with a flourish. Together, they bleated out the opening strains to "Circle of Life."

Suddenly, Lizzie wanted more than anything to stay and watch the movie with them. The movie she'd seen about a hundred times already. But she couldn't. She had to go.

"Well," she sighed. "I suppose I should leave."

Nan's expression grew soft. "We'll be fine."

"Drive safe, Mommy," Emma added, but she was clearly more interested in the DVD by now.

Okay. She wasn't needed. Emma was safe, and Lizzie had a very important, though dreaded mission to complete. Without further delay—because if she delayed, she might chicken out—she kissed her daughter again, and quickly left the room.

And hoped like hell she was doing the right thing.

Danny shifted in his seat as he waited for his dinner. This was his third evening in Butterscotch Ridge and he'd eaten every meal at the B&G. Chase's restaurant had been a pleasant surprise. Despite the slightly dated exterior, it was freshly painted and modern, though it featured antique farming tools and paintings of cows on the walls. The food choices were interesting and fresh, and the beer was cold. The only thing that struck him as odd was, whenever he walked through the door, all conversation stopped, and everyone turned to look at him. Each and every time.

It kind of set his teeth on edge, but he just turned his back on them and focused on his food.

This morning, a stranger had interrupted his breakfast, looming over him, and had asked, "'Scuse me?"

Danny had glanced up—way up—at a tall man wearing a Stetson, checkerboard shirt and actual chaps. His boots were dusty and his belt buckle was seriously enormous. A cowboy for sure. "Yeah?"

The guy tucked his thumbs in his pockets and crooked his head to the side. "You look familiar. Do you ride the circuit?"

Danny blinked. "The circuit?"

"Rodeo circuit."

Somehow, he didn't laugh. "Oh. No." Not only no, but hell, no. He'd never even been on a horse.

"Huh. I could swear I seen you somewhere before." He turned back to the bar and hollered, "Not the circuit." Some of the men at the bar groaned, but a few others cheered and collected the money lying on the bar.

Danny had brushed it off as small-town curiosity about newcomers, but he'd been here three nights and two full days and the people were still staring. And, he noticed, whispering among themselves.

Even now, there was a tall guy at the bar who kept looking over his shoulder in Danny's direction. Small town curiosity or not, he didn't like it. Fortunately, Chase appeared with his dinner just then.

"Here you go, buddy. One bacon jam burger and fries."

Danny nodded his thanks and prepared to dig in. The bacon jam burger was his favorite of anything he'd tried off the menu so far.

But rather than heading back to the kitchen, Chase dropped into the banquette across from him. Another feature of life in a small town, perhaps? "How's the hotel?" he asked.

Danny squirted ketchup on his fries and shrugged. "It's a hotel."

Chase chuckled. "Well, you're welcome to come stay at my place until Bill gets back, if you want. It's not the Ritz, but it's clean and I have cable." He grimaced. "Well, it's sorta clean."

"Thanks." As much as he appreciated the offer, getting close—to anyone in this town—was probably a mistake until he knew more about his circumstances. Aside from that, Chase had three kids and a wife. He much preferred the solitude of his single room. "I'll keep that in mind."

Chase nodded. "I get it. Just know the offer is open."

"Much appreciated."

"Well, enjoy your burger," he said, then grinned again and headed back to the bar.

As Danny watched him go, he realized he didn't mind the intrusion of his privacy as much as he thought he did. In fact, it was kind of nice to have a friend in a strange place. Granted, they'd just met, but Chase had been a better friend in a few days than some of his buddies in Vegas had been in a lifetime. That was why, in the last few years, he'd worked to weed the vampires out of his life. Especially the ones who sapped his strength, his hope and his good intentions.

It was a damn shame his mother was one of those.

When he thought about it, there was only one person in his life who had given more than she'd taken. Lizzie.

Lizzie had supported him when his mother tried to tear him down. She'd believed in him. Encouraged him. Loved him. There was a hole in his life, in his soul, where she'd once been. What he wouldn't give to see her again. Just once. Maybe talk to her. Figure out what had gone wrong. Fix it, maybe.

He knew better than to hope for that. Things had never gone easy for him. Life had never handed him anything. He'd had to work for every scrap.

Despite his mother's influence, Danny had always been an optimistic sort, believing that things always happened for a reason, and had strived to never give up. This outlook had helped him survive a very unpleasant childhood. Even as a young kid, he'd convinced himself that our trials on earth were meant to make us wiser and stronger, and therefore weren't really as cruel as they seemed at the time. But he also believed that God had a wicked sense of humor, and Danny was the butt of far too many of His jokes. Hopefully someone, somewhere, got a laugh out of all of this.

It was hardly fair, though. Because he *had* tried to find Lizzie again. Tried and tried. But it seemed as though she hadn't wanted to be found.

Chase interrupted his dismal thoughts—again—when he returned to the booth with a wicked grin, one that made Danny's neck prickle. "Well, you may be interested to know that I figured it out," he said.

Danny quirked an eyebrow. "Figured what out?"

"Why you look so familiar to everyone."

Chase waved someone over—the man at the bar who'd been watching him. He was a good-looking guy, Danny thought—tall and tanned with a slow, easy lope. They were about the same age. He was clearly another cowboy—which was no surprise.

What was a surprise was the dimple that exploded on his cheek when he smiled—a tight offering. It made something cold shimmy down Danny's spine.

Chase greeted his friend with a slap on the back. "Here he is. Danny, meet Mark." He leaned in and added, "Mark *Stirling*."

Stirling? Danny sat back and stared at the man with sharper clarity. So this was what a Stirling looked like. He stood and extended his hand. He couldn't help but notice Mark had a pretty strong grip. He tried to match it, which only made Mark's lips twitch.

Once he got his hand back, fairly uncrushed, Danny gestured to the booth. "You, uh, want to join me?"

He was surprised when both Mark and Chase nodded with alacrity, although, he noticed, they didn't bother with food. Chase just called for beers. Then, once they had their drinks, they sat there and stared at him. Neither seemed inclined to broach the subject at hand.

"All right," Danny said, taking the proverbial bull by the horns. "What's this all about?"

The two men exchanged a glance and Mark blew out a breath. "It's about the old man's will, I s'pose."

Danny lifted his bottle in a sardonic toast. Another shiver walked down his spine. "The mysterious Daniel Stirling."

"Indeed."

"Your father, I presume?"

Chase intruded with a snort. "Oh, no. His dad's been gone for, what?" He glanced at Mark. "Years."

Mark nodded. "Yeah. My dad was Daniel Junior. He passed when I was seven. The old man, our grandfather, is—was—Daniel Senior."

Danny looked down. "I'm really sorry for your loss," he said, because it seemed Mark had cared about these men, and he kind of liked Mark, even though he was coolly reserved. Then again, who wouldn't be in a situation like this?

"Thanks." Mark folded his hands and studied Danny's face some more. He glanced at Chase and shook his head. "I'm surprised it took you so long to figure out who he was."

"Not like we didn't try," Chase said. "No one caught on."

Danny cleared his throat. "Caught on to what?"

Mark grunted. "Considering he was named in the will and all."

"How would I know who was named in the will?" Chase bleated. "It's not like Bill ever lets any juicy tidbits slip." He turned to Danny. "You're named in the will," he said.

"I know."

"*I* didn't know!" For some reason, Chase sounded offended. As though he expected to be notified of everything.

Mark patted his buddy on the shoulder. "Bill is notoriously tight-lipped, as he should be. But *we* knew. The family knew. We knew *he* might be coming. We just didn't know *this*…" He waved his hand in Danny's direction, his face in particular.

Which was annoying. In fact, this whole so-called conversation was annoying. "Do you mind telling me what you're talking about?" He didn't mean to snap, but his irritation was mounting.

"The will, of course," Mark said.

"Yeah." Danny pinned him with a sharp gaze. "The will. Why would Daniel Stirling leave me anything? I never even met the guy."

"That is the question that's been raging on the ridge." Chase's smug tone made Danny grind his teeth. "See, everyone in town expected that the four Stirling grandchildren would be the only ones mentioned in the will. With the exception of Dorthea, of course."

Danny frowned. "Dorthea?"

"Daniel Senior's wife," Chase said. "The butterscotch fan. Remember?"

Mark nodded. "Our grandmother. You can imagine everyone's confusion when a stranger was mentioned in the will, too. One Daniel Diem."

"That would be me."

"It certainly would." Mark's gaze narrowed. "Naturally, we were all curious."

"I can imagine that would be...peculiar."

Mark leaned back in his seat. "But now that you're here, the reason is pretty damn clear."

That shiver returned, crawling across Danny's nape like a spider. "What is? What's pretty damn clear?" For some reason, his heart thudded. His mouth went dry.

Mark crossed his arms and fixed his gaze on Danny. "You, my friend, are the spitting image of my dad. It's pretty obvious. You are a Stirling. Through and through."

Danny gaped at him. Sure, he'd expected that Daniel Stirling might have been his long-lost and barely missed relative, but he'd never imagined that the package would come with a...sibling.

"So you're telling me you're my half brother?" And, yes, he could see the resemblance, now that he looked for it. The eyes. The nose. Maybe the mouth. Definitely the dent on the chin. Danny had always hated that dent.

"Actually, you have thrcc half brothers. And a half sister."

Danny swallowed heavily. As a kid, huddled in a grimy apartment, waiting for his mom to come home at night—if she did—he'd often wished he'd had a brother or sister. Someone to make him feel less alone in the world. He'd never dreamed it could ever happen.

And now he wasn't sure he wanted it. Wanted them.

Or to be more specific, that they wanted *him*.

Obviously, they would be resentful of his presence, of his place in the will. No matter what happened here, he was and always would be the bastard child of Daniel Stirling.

Maybe he should have stayed in Vegas after all.

Chapter Three

Danny had no idea what to say to Mark, so he was relieved when, after a short, awkward conversation, his, ahem, *brother*, excused himself with a gruff "see you tomorrow," and left.

Chase chuckled as he watched Mark hightail it out the door of the establishment. "I know where he's going."

"Yeah?"

"Straight home to tell the others. They're going to be stunned."

Danny stared at Chase for a moment, then snorted a laugh. "You think so?"

"Well, we'll see." Chase winked. "This is the biggest news that's hit town in a long while."

Great. "Do you, ah, mind keeping a lid on it for a while? Just a day or two, while I get my bearings?"

Good Lord. Danny had never seen such a melodramatic pout on a grown man. But Chase nodded. "Sure thing. I'll hold off sharing the news until tomorrow."

Well, that was something. "Thanks."

"I'll leave you to your dinner, then," he said and then he plodded back to the bar. Poor guy.

As Danny turned back to his plate, his focus shifted to the revelations he'd just encountered. He'd just met his *brother*. Well, half brother. Soon he would meet more of them. And a sister. That in itself was a lot. But he'd also learned that his father was dead. Had been dead for years, apparently. The man hadn't wanted anything to do with him. So why did Danny feel his loss so intensely?

He pushed all thoughts of *his father* from his mind and focused on what was left of his burger and fries. Naturally, his thoughts returned to Lizzie. They always did. He was wadding up his napkin and about to finish his beer and leave when a sound caught his attention. A laugh. A familiar laugh.

Heat walked through him. Without a thought, his head turned and he peered into the shadows beyond the bar. His gaze landed on a woman. He wasn't sure what it was that made the hairs on his nape prickle—the flick of her auburn hair or the movement of her body—but his lungs seized. His heart thudded.

It took an effort, but he forced himself to be calm. It couldn't be her.

Not here.

Not now.

From across the large room he could see that this woman was curvier than Lizzie had been. Her hair was longer. And the Lizzie he'd known wouldn't have been caught dead in a town like Butterscotch Ridge.

No. It couldn't be her. His imagination was just playing tricks. This was just a remnant of hope that refused to die.

He just missed her too much, he supposed. He missed everything about her. Her smile, her laugh, the warmth of her skin. And her scent. He so missed her scent. That was a strange thing to miss about a person, wasn't it? The way they smelled? But he couldn't evict the memory of the light wispy fragrance, so earthy, delicious and rare, that was so essentially Lizzie. God, he missed her. Even now, five years later, he could hardly look at another woman.

In fact, this female was the first such creature he'd even noticed—beyond the fact that they took up space in his universe.

But she wasn't Lizzie. She couldn't be, and to entertain any hope to that end would only lead to a disappointment he didn't think he could bear.

So he girded his loins, tacitly ignored her presence and focused on his plate, even though, for some reason, his appetite had vanished.

* * *

Lizzie was a bundle of nerves as she took a seat in a dim corner of the local bar and grill, aptly named the Butterscotch B&G. It was, literally, the only place in town to eat.

Butterscotch Ridge had only one hotel, too, so where to stay had been an easy decision. After checking in, she'd wandered around town a little, stretching her legs after the long drive and checking out the handful of shops—notably, a grocery store, a used bookstore and a liquor mart—before responding to the cries of her empty stomach and ending up here.

The restaurant was clean and cool, and frankly, that was all Lizzie needed right now. That, and maybe a drink. As she waited for the waitress, she tried to read the menu, but found herself wondering if she'd made a monumental mistake coming here.

Darla could have lied. Wouldn't that just be a fine kettle of fish? To be here, in this Podunk town, looking for Danny, when he could be in LA or New York or…well, anywhere?

That wasn't the only burning question, though.

She and Danny had been apart a long time. She'd certainly changed since then. But what would he be like now? Had he married, or did he still manage to deftly skirt commitment? What would it be like to see him again? More to the point, how would he react to her news? What heartbreak would this weekend bring?

If she even found him. *If* he was even here.

"Hey there." A glass of ice water appeared before her and Lizzie glanced up to see a cheerful waitress in a bright apron brandishing her pad. "My name's Crystal. What can I get you?"

"Oh." Lizzie leaned back and sighed. "A lemon drop would be awesome."

"Lemon drop?" Crystal chuckled. "I'm afraid that's way beyond our bartender's pay grade. May I suggest a rum and Coke?" She leaned closer and winked. "It comes with a maraschino cherry. No extra charge."

Lizzie bit back a grin. "Sounds awesome." It would be nice to wash the dust of the trip from her throat. Or maybe there was something else drying her mouth. Something that tasted like angst.

"Perfect." Crystal scribbled on her pad. "You want to eat, too?"

"Yes, but not yet." Lizzie waved the menu. "I'm still looking. Anything you recommend?"

"Steaks are good."

Lizzie grimaced. She wasn't much of a carnivore. "Anything lighter?"

"We have some nice salads." Crystal pointed to that section of the menu. But before Lizzie could scope them out, the waitress said, "We don't get many strangers here. Usually just regulars." It was a gentle prodding, but Lizzie didn't bite.

"This seems like a nice place," she said, glancing around the well-kept interior.

Crystal chuckled. "Oh, it's quiet now. All family-style and proper. You should see it when the week-end really gets started. After the dinner hour, this place becomes a bona fide honky-tonk."

"I'll have to check it out." She wouldn't. Honky-tonk was hardly her style. "How long have you lived here?" she asked.

Crystal rolled her eyes. "Forever."

"You like it?"

"Oh, yeah. It's peaceful. There's a real community—the people are the best."

"That's good to know." She put down the menu and pinned Crystal with a curious gaze. She seemed friendly and chatty, so Lizzie decided she might as well just ask the question hovering on her tongue. "Have you ever met someone named Daniel Diem?"

She wasn't prepared in the least for Crystal's response. Her eyes widened and she issued a little *eep*. "*Danny* Diem? Of course, I know him." She leaned in and whispered, "Generous tipper."

"Really?" Lizzie gaped at her. Was it really that easy? Just waltz in and ask a random stranger? Apparently, it was just that easy. In Butterscotch Ridge, at least.

"In fact, I just saw him having supper."

Lizzie's heart gave a hard thump. A million thoughts and emotions whipped through her, including an exhilarating mix of terror and elation. After everything she'd been through, now, finally, all her hopes and fears would be answered once and for all.

Crystal scanned the establishment. "Yeah. There he is." She pointed across the bar into the restaurant.

Lizzie's gut clenched.

Time seemed to slow as she turned her head to follow Crystal's gaze. She froze as her glance fell on the too-handsome man, who was staring back at her from across the restaurant. There was no doubt in her mind that it was Danny. Sure, he was a little older, but she'd know that muscled silhouette, the cut of that chin, anywhere.

Apparently, she'd deluded herself to think that she'd forgotten all about him, wiped him from her psyche, cleansed him from her heart. But she'd been wrong. Really, really wrong.

It all came flooding back in the fraction of a second. She remembered his laugh, his kisses, the way he made her feel safe and wanted in his arms. She remembered…everything.

Their gazes clashed. As she stood, so did he.

Five and a half years was a long time. She'd certainly changed since then—gone from being a girl with no worries to a woman with a world of responsibilities on her shoulders. Had he grown up at all?

One thing she knew for sure—he still made her heart patter. He also made her mind turn to mush. Which was definitely not good. The last thing she wanted was to have this conversation with him while she was in such an emotional state. But she had no choice, did she?

It seemed to take forever for her to cross the room to him. Up close, he was so striking, so familiar, the sight nearly brought her to tears. The lines of his face hadn't changed much, though his dark hair had begun to silver a whisper. His eyes were the same, though. Warm and brown and wreathed in thick lashes. Memories engulfed her. The good ones. Not the ones she tried to bring to mind whenever she was foolish enough to miss him, those thorny memories of a man who wanted nothing more than playtime. A man who'd not been ready or willing for the responsibility of a family.

"Danny."

The sound of her voice seemed to shock him from his stupor. "Lizzie? Is it really you?"

"Yes."

"What—what are you doing here?" His tone was sharp. As though he was shocked and displeased to see her. She'd expected as much, but frankly hadn't expected it would hurt this badly.

She tipped up her chin. "I came here to find you."

A dark eyebrow arched, sending shivers down her spine. "How did you know where I was?"

"I, ah…" Heat rose on her cheeks. "I called around. Darla told me you were coming to Butterscotch Ridge."

"Darla." Not a snort, but just barely. "How the hell did she know?"

"She said she heard from Rob."

A muscle ticked in his cheek. "What did she tell you?"

"Just that you were coming here."

"Did she say why?"

Lizzie lifted a shoulder. "That you have some kind of inheritance."

She was not prepared for the mask that closed over his features. It frightened her. He narrowed his eyes and frowned.

When he didn't respond—at all—awkwardness descended. The worst awkwardness she'd ever experienced. And she had no idea how to dispel it. Not with him standing there, arms crossed, staring at her coldly.

He broke the silence with four sharp words. "Why are you here?"

"Why don't you sit down?" She did so herself, sliding into the banquette of his booth—her knees were about to give in, anyway.

He ignored her request. "Why are you here?"

"Danny, this is hard enough, and you're not making it any easier for me—"

"Oh, *I'm* not making it easier for you? You're the one who left me. No warning. Nothing. Just... gone. Poof."

Irritation bubbled, and though she'd told herself she wouldn't allow her anger to surface, she couldn't help snapping, "There was plenty of warning. You weren't paying attention."

"Really? I was sure paying attention during our last fight. I remember that pretty clearly."

"Do you? Do you remember what we fought about?"

His face went blank and he dropped into his seat where he could face her, but not come too close. As though he were protecting himself from her.

What a laugh. She was the one who needed protecting. He was far too addictive for her own good.

"Why don't you tell me what you remember?" he suggested.

She sighed. "We'd been talking about the future."

"Ah, yes." He settled back into his seat, his expression still mutinous.

"And you freaked out."

He frowned. "I did not *freak out*."

"You made it pretty clear we had no future together."

"I didn't say that. I just said I didn't want marriage."

"Or kids."

"And can you blame me? With parents like mine? What kind of father would I be?"

That comment hit her like a blow. Stole her breath. Made her question her own sanity for coming here.

Nothing had changed. Nothing had changed at all.

"And my mother?" he continued harshly. "Did Darla tell you what my mother has done now?"

"She said she skipped bail."

He barked a bitter laugh. "Skipped bail, then skipped town. But before she disappeared, she cleaned out my bank accounts and my apartment. She hocked everything I own. Everything I've worked for."

Anger raged in Lizzie's heart. The woman truly had no moral compass.

"You're *not* like your mother." She'd told him that a thousand times, but too many years raised by that horrible woman had clouded his self-image.

"And then, there's the father. The man who wanted nothing to do with me. The man who wouldn't even acknowledge my existence. He certainly didn't support us."

"You're not like him, either." She hoped…

He shook his head and scrubbed his face with his palms. "It doesn't matter. None of that matters. Not anymore." She hated his expression, the resignation and the pain. "So, why are you here?" The question again, this time, whispered.

She might as well just dive in. "I…need your help."

He frowned again. "What do you want?"

Her heart stuttered. Oh, Lord. Now that the time was here, she didn't know what to say. Or how to say it. Or anything.

Danny waited, silently, watching her. Then his lips tweaked into a hint of a sad smile. "You're procrastinating, Lizzie. You never procrastinate unless it's something bad."

Her expression must have given something away because he paled.

"Are you okay? Are you sick?"

She shook her head. "I'm fine. And no. It's not bad. Not bad at all. Well, not all bad. There is some bad, I suppose. But it's…" She trailed off. She was babbling—she knew she was. It was yet another way she avoided unpleasant topics.

Danny pinned her with a sharp look. "What is it you want to tell me?"

She wrinkled her nose. "About that last fight we had—"

"What about it?" His tone was tight, as though the words were bitter on his tongue.

Right. "The one where you told me you didn't want marriage or children." She tried not to sound bitter, as well, but failed.

"For good reason," he snapped.

"Right," she snapped right back. Then she met his gaze as bravely as she could. "Well, I was pregnant."

Lizzie's words hit Danny like a tidal wave. All kinds of emotions swamped him, so many that he couldn't separate them, couldn't make sense of them. Couldn't…anything.

He stared at her. "Pregnant?" The moment passed

in a sizzle of silence and then he asked, because he had to, "Was it mine?"

Her expression froze, then crumbled, which hit him like a punch to the chest. He hadn't meant to hurt her, but he had. Clearly he had. After a moment, she composed herself, tipped up her chin in that way she had when she was infuriated and said, "Seriously? Are you asking me that?"

"I think I deserve to know." She should know as much, as adamant as he'd been against being a father.

In response, she pulled out her phone. He didn't understand the move at first, but then she turned it to him and he saw.

Oh, God. He saw.

It was a picture of an adorable cherub with a heart-shaped face, bright brown eyes and a toss of dark curls. The dent in her chin even matched his. She was a perfect and exquisite mix of the two of them. There was no doubt about that. Danny's heart thudded and his lungs locked as he stared at the image.

His daughter. This was his *daughter*.

He had a child.

Some strange and great elation rolled through him at the sight of her. It made him giddy and filled with joy. What a pity it was quickly followed by dread and fury as the facts clicked into place. "Why didn't you tell me?"

Lizzie looked away. "I tried to tell you that night."

"But you didn't." And it hurt. It hurt like hell that she'd kept such an enormous secret from him. Never mind it was a secret he would have rejected back then.

She sighed and raked back her hair. He tried not to notice how vulnerable she was, how pale, how beautiful. "I don't know what I was trying to do. Maybe get you to say you wanted more with me. To try and feel more secure in my relationship with you before I told you about the baby. I didn't want you to be with me because you felt obligated."

"Obligated?" Apparently, he was so stunned, all he could do was repeat the last word she said.

"Anyway, when I said what I said, and you said what you said… I decided to leave. I decided I would raise the baby by myself, rather than tie you down and make you resent both of us."

"I would never have—"

"But you would have. Come on, Danny. With the mindset you were in? You would have."

He let the argument drop, because she was probably right. He'd been pretty self-absorbed back then.

Too bad he still was sometimes.

He sucked in a deep breath and forced himself to calm. "So… You're sure she's mine?"

It was clear she was trying not to roll her eyes—he knew her that well. "We can do a paternity test, if you like. But honestly, Danny, I'm not asking you to step in and be a dad—"

"You don't want me to be a part of her life?" he interjected, somehow wounded by her words. Somehow more determined than ever to prove her wrong.

"Only if you want to."

Oh, he wanted to. He didn't know why, but he did. "I have a child." It took everything in him to form those words, so alien to his nature. So frightening.

She smiled then, and it was a lovely smile that made his chest hurt. "Her name is Emma."

Emma.

"Pretty name."

"After my mother." She looked down at her hands. "I hope you don't mind."

It was all he could do not to snort. They sure as hell wouldn't have named her after his. "So she's… five?"

Lizzie nodded. Right. They'd been apart five and a half years.

He forced down his anger. She was right that he'd been a selfish jerk back then, but that didn't wash away his resentment. Still, there was something more important here than his disgruntlement, or his fear or his conviction that he'd be a horrible parent.

Emma.

"What…?" What to ask? "What's she like?"

Lizzie smiled. Her defenses softened. "She's a

little like me. A lot like you." She waved at the picture. "She has your hair, your eyes and, well, to be honest, your stubbornness." Lizzie chuckled a little. Her expression was enraptured; her love for her daughter shone through her eyes. "She's a funny little thing. Always saying things you don't expect. And she's clever. She loves puzzles and math and knows all the words to every Disney song."

"Really?"

"Oh yes. *Every one*." A laugh. "She's a smart one, our Emma." She stilled abruptly, as though she'd realized what she'd just said and regretted it.

Danny decided to let that go because one thought, and one thought only, swirled in his mind. "Does she want to meet me?"

Lizzie's head whipped up. She gaped at him in horror. *"What?"*

"Does she want to meet me? Is that why you're here?"

"No. No! She doesn't even know you exist."

Why did that fact gut him like a fish? Irritation rippled and some unfamiliar possessive instinct raised its ugly head and roared. "She doesn't know I *exist*?"

"Well, she knows she has a sperm donor—"

"A sperm donor?" He should probably try to remain calm, but somehow, being referred to as nothing more than a sperm donor was deeply disturbing.

"Yes."

"How on earth does she know that?"

"She has a bad habit." Lizzie sighed. "She likes to eavesdrop on adult conversations."

His pulse ticked. "You refer to me as the sperm donor?"

"I… Sometimes."

"I want to meet her." Where this urge came from he had no clue, but he knew it, felt it, needed it to the core of his being.

Lizzie studied him for a moment or two, as though assessing his sincerity. And then she nodded. "Good. Because we need you."

Something cold slithered through his veins, probably from the hint of desperation in her tone. "You *need* me? Suddenly, after five years?"

"Yes." She nodded and dropped her gaze to her fingers, which, he noticed, were tangled on the tabletop and white from strain. "You see, Emma's sick. And without your help, she may die."

Danny's world—just newly formed—suddenly shattered. "What does that mean, she's sick?"

Lizzie cleared her throat. "It all started about a year ago. She started bruising, badly. And then she got sick. Real sick. A cold developed into pneumonia within days. I—I thought I was going to lose her." Lizzie's eyes glistened with tears, and she swiped at them. Danny's heart ached for her. He should have been there for her. He could have…

Impulsively, he covered her hand with his. "What was the diagnosis?"

"It's a thing called aplastic anemia. I'd never

heard of it. Basically, it's…sort of a bone-marrow failure."

His heart lurched. "Cancer?"

Lizzie shook her head. "No. I'm not explaining it well." She took a deep breath. "Her bone marrow doesn't make enough white blood cells, so she can't fight infections. She's tired a lot because she doesn't make enough red blood cells. She can't form platelets to stop excessive bleeding…"

"Can't they give her blood transfusions?"

Lizzie huffed a cynical laugh. "We've tried that. They have to give her drugs to suppress her immune system when they do, so she gets even sicker. We've tried almost everything." She sighed. "Nothing has worked."

"What do you need from me?"

She turned to him and held his gaze. "She needs a bone-marrow transplant. Stem cells, preferably. I'm incompatible. I was hoping you would…"

"Give her bone marrow?" He'd heard about that. He'd heard it hurt. A lot. He had no idea why he immediately ignored that consideration. "Of course."

"It's not that easy. You have to be tested first to see if you're a match…" She hesitated. "You might not be."

He didn't like that prospect in the least. "Why not? I'm her father."

"I thought the same thing at first. But I'm her mother, and I'm not a match. The doctors say related donors are the best. They suggested I reach out to you because, Danny, you might be her last hope for a related donor."

Wow. That comment hit him hard. Panic and fear swirled in his chest, but he tried to push them away. Panic and fear never solved anything.

All that mattered now was Emma.

Damn. He never expected caring about someone elsc—someone he'd never met—could hurt this much.

But it did hurt. He was, in a word, eviscerated.

How could this be? How could he feel such desperation over a child whose existence had been unknown to him just a few minutes ago?

If this was parenting, it was gut-wrenching.

Resolve formed in his chest. Damn it, he would be the best dad he could be. No matter how terrible his own parents had been, he would not fail Emma.

He stood, took both Lizzie's hands and pulled her to her feet. "Listen. We're going to figure this out. And I'm going to be here, right by your side, okay?"

She peered up at him through the tears, and said, in a tiny voice, "Okay."

"Whatever it takes, whatever Emma needs, we'll make it happen. Do you hear me?"

"Yes."

"You're not alone anymore, Lizzie. I'm in this with you. All the way."

He had no idea where these words were coming from. He'd never uttered anything like this before. But he'd never *felt* this way before, either.

As frightening as all this was, he was determined to come through for his child. And for Lizzie.

And when she wrapped her arms around him and whispered, "Thank you, Danny," he knew he'd done the right thing.

Chapter Four

As she retook her seat across from him, Lizzie struggled to collect herself. She'd been prepared to defend her decision to keep Emma from him... but it hadn't been necessary at all.

He'd straight up accepted the fact that he was Emma's father—albeit through a veil of shock—and then he'd agreed immediately to do whatever was necessary. He'd pledged to be with her, by her side. She wouldn't have to face this alone anymore—a prospect that had overwhelmed her with emotion.

What more could she have asked? Had she really agonized over this, certain that facing Danny would only make things worse?

She peeked at him from beneath her lashes. His

expression was determined, his chin was hard, his jaw clenched, and it hit her.

This was a man. Not a boy. Not a feckless kid. A man.

He had grown up.

She swallowed heavily as a whisper of trepidation trickled through her veins. She'd been head over heels in love with Danny five years ago, even though she was well aware of his faults and foibles. How on earth was she going to protect her heart against him now? Knowing her arguments against him were slipping away? Knowing that he was willing to stay by her side? At least until Emma was better.

Crystal chose this moment to appear at their booth, delivering Lizzie's drink. She grinned at them both. "I see you found each other."

Egads. What a statement. In fact, it was so surreal, Lizzie chuckled. Somehow, that broke the tension between them and Danny grinned, as well.

A shiver skittered up Lizzie's spine. How she'd missed that smile. With that explosion of dimples, his cheek should be registered as a lethal weapon.

"We did," he said. The fact that he reached across the table and covered her hand with his sent a delicious warmth coursing through her.

She tamped down the feeling. This was no time for lust.

"Have you decided what you want?" Crystal asked.

It took a second for Lizzie to realize she was talking about food, because her mind immediately whipped to a picture of her and Danny and Emma, together. That was what she wanted. It was what she'd always wanted, even if she'd told herself otherwise. It was a foolish thought, but maybe she was a fool.

"Um, the chicken salad, I think." In truth, she wasn't hungry anymore, but knew if she didn't eat something, she'd regret it later tonight.

"Right away." Crystal turned to Danny. "Can I get you anything else?"

He blew out a breath. "I could use another beer."

Lizzie blinked. He'd never been much of a beer man. "Not something stronger?"

There was humor in his eyes when he responded. "I don't think that would be wise, given the circumstances." And then, when she sent him a curious glance, he added, "We need to have a serious discussion."

Right. Of course.

Crystal nodded and headed off, and Danny released Lizzie's hand. She missed his warmth immediately. "Where, uh, where shall we start?" she asked.

He picked up his beer, swirled the dregs and shrugged. "How about, where did you go?"

It was a simple question, but she felt a hint of pain and fury behind it, although he was trying to keep it in check.

"Seattle."

His lids flickered, but he didn't respond, leaving a silent abyss between them.

"My sister, Nan, she took me in. Helped me get a job with a good firm. Everything was...fine, until Emma got sick last year."

Then it had become the worst time of her life.

"And it didn't occur to you to contact me even then?"

She dropped her gaze. "No."

Again, he didn't respond. He didn't move until she looked up again. "Why?" The question, a simple word, seemed squeezed up from the core of his soul. The agony in his tone made tears prick at her lids. "Did you hate me so much?" he asked tightly.

"I never hated you." It was true. She'd been angry and hurt and totally confused, but there had never been hate for him in her heart. "I just..."

"What?" He stared at her with eyes so like Emma's, it was painful to hold his gaze.

"I was sure you would..." Ah, how to say it without crushing him?

"I would refuse to accept her?"

She sighed and mangled her napkin. "There was that fear, yes."

He sat back, his eyes wreathed in those sinfully thick lashes, his brows furrowed. "Is that what you think of me?" He tossed back his beer, only to realize it was empty.

"I didn't know how you would react. You've never been shy about your aversion to parenthood."

He was silent for a minute, then he cleared his throat and said, "Well, that's all behind us now, isn't it?"

She shook her head, struggling to make this quantum shift with him. "Is it?"

"Yes." He met her gaze. His was calm, cool and determined. "Emma is what's important here. Her health. Her safety. She's all that matters."

Oh, dear God.

Relief, unlike any she'd ever known, sluiced through her. Relief and…elation. Knowing that they were united, that this would not be a fight, was a sweet respite from the unspoken worry that had been torturing her since she'd made the decision to find him. That and the tacit forgiveness for keeping this secret from him. That worry had tormented her, as well.

There were no words to adequately express her gratitude. A simple, heartfelt "Thank you, Danny," would have to do.

He nodded, and they eased into silence as Crystal appeared with her salad and another beer for Danny. He waited until Lizzie had eaten a bit before he said, "So, what do we do now?"

Oh, dear. She hadn't thought that far ahead. Not really. What did they do now? Head back to Seattle for a family reunion?

Even though he'd been wonderful about this, a

part of her was still nervous over how Emma might react to meeting her father, the man heretofore referred to as *the sperm donor*. Emma deserved to meet him, certainly. She deserved to know him, and he deserved the same, but Lizzie was oddly hesitant to rush things.

She shrugged. "Get you tested."

"I mean about Emma."

Oh. Yes. "Take things slow, I guess."

He set his chin in a stubborn gesture she knew by heart. "I want to meet her."

"What about your business here in Butterscotch Ridge?"

His eyebrows lowered. "I think my *daughter's health* is more important." The vehemence in his voice warmed her heart. It was what she'd been hoping he would say, because it was what she would have said. But then he added, "I can always meet my family later."

She gaped at him. "Your...*what*?"

"Oh." He shook his head. "Yeah. Apparently I'm the bastard grandson of a local rancher. Just met my *brother*, if you can believe that." She couldn't help noticing the flush on his cheeks, the restlessness of his fingers, his general discomfort.

"That must have been a shock."

He caught her gaze and blew out a breath, then gave her a hint of a smile. "This has been some kind of day."

The enormity of it overwhelmed even her. To

discover you had not only a child, but also an entire family...

"To be honest, I'm ready to go see Emma now." Lizzie's gut clenched. He must have noticed her expression grow pale because he leaned in. "What?"

She forced a smile. "What?"

He leaned back and blew out a breath. "Come on, Lizzie. I know you too well. Do you not want me to meet her?"

Yes. Somehow he'd managed to hit the nail on the head. Well, not precisely on the head, but thereabouts. "It's just that..."

He waited for her to finish, and when she delayed too long, he drummed his fingers on the tabletop. "Well?"

Oh, God. She prayed for strength. "It's just that... I need time. To prepare her."

To his credit, he didn't respond with anger, as she expected. It had been five years, after all. She'd had five years to prepare Emma for this moment. But she hadn't done it. She hadn't done anything.

He folded his hands and stared at them as though they held the secrets of the universe. "Okay," he said finally. "How much time do you need?"

She swallowed heavily. How much time? She had no idea. "Don't you have business here?"

"It's just the reading of a will—"

"And meeting your family. Isn't that what you said?"

Danny grimaced. "I think I made my opinion

about all that pretty clear. Nothing matters besides Emma."

"All right. Would you give me a couple days? Please?"

The muscle in his jaw worked as he considered the offer, and then he nodded.

She nearly collapsed in relief. "If I leave tomorrow, I can make arrangements for you to come on, say, Tuesday?"

He clearly didn't want to wait until Tuesday, but he agreed. Then, his stark expression melted into something else. "I can't wait to meet her," he said softly, a light shining in his eyes.

She had to smile back. "You'll adore her."

"I know," he said, giving her hand a squeeze. "I already do."

After dinner, Danny and Lizzie walked together back to the hotel where they were both staying. It almost felt like a date. Neither wanted to turn in, so they sat together in the lounge that doubled as a breakfast bar and talked late into the night, just catching up. Just getting to know each other again. And of course, talking about Emma.

They made plans to meet for breakfast before she left for Seattle and then he walked her to her room and waited in the hall until her door closed to make sure she was safe. Then he returned to his room just down the hall.

He wouldn't be sleeping. He knew he wouldn't

be. How could he, with Lizzie just a couple rooms away? How could he, with all the thoughts rumbling through his mind?

He must have slept, though, because the next morning, far too early, Danny was awakened by a call from the lawyer's secretary letting him know that Watney was back in town, and would see him this morning at 8:00 a.m. sharp.

Danny had no idea why this summons gave him a stomachache, but it did. His first thought was to tell Lizzie, so he headed straight for her room. And damn, he woke her up. She looked cute when she was all disheveled.

"What are you smiling at?" she muttered, pushing her hair out of her eyes.

"Good morning."

"Is it?"

"I just got a call from the lawyer."

She stilled. Her eyes widened.

"He wants to meet with me at eight o'clock. What time were you planning to leave?"

"Right after breakfast. Just to try and avoid the weekend traffic heading back to the city."

"Would you…?" Dang. How to ask? "Would you be willing to wait until after this meeting?" He wasn't sure it was fair to ask her to stay so he would have someone to discuss all this with, but he really needed her. More than he ever had. "I know it's a big imposition, but since I have literally no idea what's going to happen, I'd really appreciate having someone I know nearby. Hopefully it'll just be an extra hour or so. We can have lunch instead of breakfast. If that's okay."

He was relieved beyond words when she said yes. "Thank you, Lizzie," he said. "Thank you so much."

She nodded and then, as he turned to go, she caught his hand and brought him back for a quick hug. "Good luck," she said.

"Thanks." And yeah, though he appreciated it, that hug was way too short.

Danny grabbed a muffin from the breakfast bar as he headed out of the hotel. It was stale, but did the job of filling his stomach, which was churning a bit. His steps lagged as he made his way down Main Street. And not just because he was walking away from a disheveled Lizzie. His mind lagged, as well. He wasn't ready for this, whatever it was going to be. The last thing he wanted was to have to deal with disgruntled siblings. Not with worries about Emma and hopes about Lizzie crowding his mind.

It surprised him, the relief that flooded him as he saw Mark hop out of his truck in front of Watney's offices. Ah. A familiar face. "Good morning," he called with a friendly wave.

"I take it you got a call from Watney, too?" he asked.

"Yup." Mark clapped him on the shoulder. "Are you ready for this?"

"No," Danny said on a huffed breath.

Mark chuckled as he stepped up on Watney's

porch and opened the door to a rather grand-looking establishment. As Danny stepped into the lobby it struck him that the offices resembled an old-timey bordello, decorated with thickly upholstered gilt furniture and red velvet wall coverings. All the wood gleamed and the scent of beeswax hovered in the air.

An older woman with too much lipstick and a beehive hairdo sat at an ornately scrolled cherry-wood desk that blocked the entrance—apparently, it was meant to be a bastion against intruders.

Mark greeted her with a noisy kiss to her powdered cheek. "Well, good morning, Gladys," he said in a warm voice.

"Mark Stirling," she gushed. "You're such a lady killer, just like your pa."

"Gladys. Look who I found," Mark said, pulling Danny forward. "Danny, this is Gladys Henry. She makes some of the best lemonade in town. Brings it to every July Fourth picnic."

Gladys stilled as she gazed at Danny. Her eyes widened and her mouth dropped open as she looked him over. And then she picked up her phone, pressed the intercom button and gushed, "He's here, Mr. Watney! He's here." Then she slammed down the receiver and fanned herself.

"Amazing, isn't it?" Mark asked, leaning a hip against the desk.

Gladys renewed her avid perusal of his person. "Astounding. Absolutely astounding. It's like stepping back in time." She fluttered her lashes at Danny. "I always had such a hankering for Daniel Junior, you know."

No. He hadn't known. And frankly, it was a little uncomfortable to hear, since he'd never known a thing about his father until yesterday…except that the man hadn't given a damn about him his entire life.

Gladys's open stare was a little uncomfortable, too.

The awkward tableau was shattered when a rotund bear of a man, with an imposing handlebar mustache and actual muttonchops, burst into the waiting room from the offices in the back. "Who's here, Gladys? For pity sake. Couldn't you be more…?"

His words trailed off when he saw Danny and more gaping ensued. Honestly, if it was going to be like this with everyone he met, he might just walk back to Vegas now.

"Hello, young man," he said at long last, thrusting out a hand. "I'm Bill Watney. Welcome. Right on time, I see. We…ah…need to wait for everyone else to arrive."

Everyone? The thought sent prickles up his nape.

"Mark, why don't you take Daniel to the meeting room while I collect the papers?"

"Sure thing, sir." Mark nodded his head at Danny as he led the way. "Come on. More comfortable in here."

Frankly, the meeting room didn't look any more comfortable—it was easily as fancy as the entrance, if not more—but it had the benefit of privacy. Or at least the pretense of it. When Mark closed the door behind them, Danny shook his head. "I never imagined my presence could cause such a kerfuffle."

He shrugged. "Life moves slower here. Some of us have more time to gossip than we ought."

Small town life. Awesome.

The two men sat for a while in the plush room, sharing small talk and sipping the lemonade Gladys brought them, along with the news that Samantha, *the sister*, was on her way. It was a pleasant respite for Danny, who was still beset with thoughts of Lizzie and Emma, and struggled to embrace the surreal fact that he had…a *family*.

It was clear Mark was doing all he could to make Danny feel at home, which was damn nice. A far cry from the rancorous welcome he'd expected.

But when he heard a female voice in the other room, his tranquility fled. He leaped to his feet and faced the door, his heart thudding and his stomach in a knot.

He was about to meet his sister. Half sister.

Why was that such a terrifying prospect?

The door swung open and Samantha Stirling stepped through. Though short in stature, and rather petite compared to Mark's bulk, it was clear she was a force to be reckoned with. Her jet-black hair was cut in a long bob that complemented her heart-shaped face. Her eyes were wide and bright and blue, fringed by dark lashes, and she had that signature dent in her chin. Her expression was fierce. She was, in a word, intimidating.

She stared at him for a moment, looked him up and down, crossed her arms over her chest and then…grunted.

Mark chuckled. "Get it now?"

In response, she glared at her brother. "I'm not a complete idiot."

"So you say."

Pointedly, she turned her back on Mark and thrust out a hand. "I'm Samantha, but everyone calls me Sam. Welcome, Daniel," she said in a tone that was decidedly unwelcoming. But Danny couldn't blame her.

"He goes by Danny," Mark interjected.

"Danny." She studied him some more and then said, "Where are you staying?"

The conversational pivot caught him off guard. He'd expected a grilling of a completely different kind. "Um…at the hotel in town?"

"The hotel?" Her ferocity took him aback. "You're not staying *there*."

Danny blinked and glanced at Mark, who shrugged.

She whirled back to Mark. "He's staying at the house."

"Uh, I'm okay at a hotel. I don't want to be a bother." A lie. He could hardly afford the hotel. At least, not for a prolonged stay.

Sam snorted. "I'm not having the entire town think you're not welcome under our roof." Again, she spoke with distinct pique.

"The house is huge," Mark said. "You'll be much more comfortable there. Plus, it will give us all a chance to get to know each other better."

"Are you sure the others won't mind?" Danny asked.

Sam rolled her eyes. "It hardly matters. As a family, we need to present a unified front." She didn't say it, but Danny could hear the unspoken part of the sentence. *Whether we want to or not.*

"Great. It's settled then," Mark said cheerfully.

"What's settled?" A gravelly voice filled the room, and Danny turned to see the entryway shadowed by two more enormous men, dwarfing an old woman between them.

When the men's gazes landed on him, he wanted to shrink into the floor. And he'd thought Sam was intimidating? Holy hell.

The taller man's eyes narrowed and little lines crinkled around his mouth in a way that telegraphed his displeasure. The other man, only slightly less tall, had a similar response, which was only a little more menacing due to the scar traversing his right cheek.

They both remained silent.

The tiny woman between them, however, did not. She broke the awkward pause by scurrying forward with a sprightliness that belied her age and, avoiding all efforts to corral her to the safer side of the room, rushed into Danny's arms.

Well, not his arms per se, because he hadn't been prepared for a hug. Other than that far too-brief embrace with Lizzie this morning, no one had hugged him in a long time.

But this woman did. She smelled of lilacs and perfumed soap, which was, to his surprise, kind of comforting. She seemed both frail and ferocious.

"Daniel. You've finally come home." She took his hand and led him to the divan, oblivious of her guardian's glowers. Then again, the glowers were meant for Danny. However, had he been of the mind to refuse her guidance, he doubt he could have broken away from that iron grip. Once they were seated, side by side, she patted him incessantly and prattled on about how thrilled she was to see him.

All while the two men glared at him.

Mark, once again, saved him. "Danny, this is Dorthea, our grandmother. And these are our other brothers. This is DJ." He nodded to the taller one, who stiffened slightly in greeting.

"My name is Daniel Stirling the third," he said. "Most people call me DJ." He lifted an eyebrow. "Given the circumstances, I think we should stick to that."

O-o-okay. Danny couldn't help thinking DJ's tone could have iced a beer.

But Mark wasn't done introducing surly people

yet. "And this is your other brother Luke." He gestured to the scarred sibling.

"Uh…nice to meet you guys," Danny said with a nod.

"*Half* brother," Luke muttered.

"None of that. Remember?" Sam snapped. "We agreed. A united front."

Luke blew out a breath and raked back his hair, revealing more scars. Danny forced away his gaze. It probably wouldn't help the situation to stare.

But what would help this situation?

"Look," he said to everyone, "I'm only here because I was asked to come. I don't want to cause any trouble. As soon as all this is wrapped up, I'll be on my way."

He had no idea why DJ and Luke exchanged a sarcastic glance.

Or maybe he did.

Maybe that was what they would expect of an outsider. To sweep in, rake up some cash and be gone.

Which was the plan, so there was no need for that little ping of pain in his chest, was there? Why should he care what they thought of him?

But somehow, even though he'd only just met them, he did.

"Oh, look, Bill," Dorthea warbled as William Watney entered the room juggling a stack of papers. "Daniel has come home."

Watney glanced from Dorthea to Danny and

nodded. "How nice." He dropped his burden onto the cherrywood desk at the far end of the room. "Shall we begin?"

"Please," DJ said crisply.

As DJ was the one the lawyer had addressed, Danny realized that, in this family, he was the leader of the pack and he filed that bit of information away.

"Excellent." The others all sat. Danny couldn't help noticing Luke's limp as he made his way to a chair. Watney cleared his throat in a way that made his wattle wobble. "Ahem. As you all know, Daniel Stirling Senior had a very particular belief about life—"

"Here we go," Luke muttered.

Watney sent him a quelling glance, but given the mustache and muttonchops, Danny was doubtful he made his point.

"At any rate, he has always been very particular about the importance of family." He paused and glanced at each of them in turn, as though waiting for some other rebellion. When it was not forthcoming, he continued. "This belief is reflected in his will." Watney fished through the papers and pulled out an official-looking document. "In short, he has left everything to his five living heirs, to be split equally, five ways—"

"Isn't that sweet?" Dorthea cooed.

"What?" Luke bellowed. "*Five* ways?" He glared

at Danny. "How do we even know he is who he says he is?"

Which got Danny's dander up. Without thinking, he sprang to his feet. "Now wait a damn minute. *He's* the one who asked me here." He pointed at Watney, who rolled his eyes. "Last week, I didn't even have a clue that any of you existed, which, quite frankly, was fine with me."

Luke leaped to his feet, as well. "Are we not even going to ask for a blood test?" he asked the room at large.

Watney raised his hand, asking for silence, perhaps. Everyone ignored him.

"You want a blood test?" Danny bellowed. Somehow they were now nose-to-nose. "I'll give you a damned blood test."

"Both of you, sit down," Watney hollered. Though they continued to glower at each other, both Danny and Luke took their seats. Once they were settled again, the lawyer continued. "A blood test, in this situation, is irrelevant."

Danny's pulse thudded. "What?"

Everyone's attention swiveled back to the man with all the information.

"What do you mean?" DJ asked.

Watney shrugged. "A blood test is irrelevant, from a legal standpoint. Daniel Diem is named in the will as an heir. He's not named as a grandchild, so whether he is Stirling blood or not doesn't matter. He's an heir, just like all of you."

"That's ridiculous," Luke growled. "I demand a blood test."

Sam frowned. "You know what it will tell us. Look at his face." She waved in Danny's direction.

"I don't care. I want his DNA."

"Calm down," DJ barked. He nodded at Watney to continue.

The lawyer harrumphed a little, as old-time lawyers tended to do, and then repeated himself. "Your grandfather has left everything to his five living heirs, to be split equally. The only codicil is that all five heirs must work at the ranch for a period of three years before receiving their inheritance."

Danny's heart jerked. Three years? Trapped here? But what about Emma? What about Lizzie?

"Son of a—" Luke bounded to his feet and began to pace, his limp even more pronounced. "He's still doing it. Even from beyond the grave. That man can't help but control every damned thing!"

Sam was more prosaic in her reaction. She frowned at the lawyer. "What if one of the heirs doesn't want to stay three years and work on the ranch?" And, yes, her gaze skittered to Danny.

Watney looked down at the papers, but more to avoid her gaze than anything else.

"Well?" DJ asked.

The lawyer fiddled with his mustache for a few moments and then sighed. "He was very clear that you must all work on the ranch. And if any one of you refuses to adhere to the terms of the will, the ranch in its entirety reverts to…Johnson Cage."

A heavy silence fell. And then, all hell broke loose.

All the Stirlings leaped to their feet and began talking at once. All except Mark, who threw back his head and laughed…bitterly.

Luke mostly swore because, apparently, he had no intention of staying in this godforsaken town for three years and Sam turned to DJ to ask if they had the assets to buy *someone* out. For his part, DJ tried to calm everyone down, to no avail.

"Who is Johnson Cage?" Danny asked when the hubbub had quieted enough to be heard.

"Who is Johnson Cage?" Luke snarled.

DJ cleared his throat. "He was our grandfather's partner—"

"Ex-partner," Sam said with vitriol.

"They had a falling-out. Decades ago. Split the ranch in half," Mark explained. "Never spoke again."

"He hated Johnson Cage." Sam shook her head. "Why would he do this?"

"Don't you get it?" Luke snarled. "It's just his way. He can't bear for us to have any peace. Even after death he feels obliged to control us."

As the conversation roiled around him, Danny's mind spun. Part of him registered the fact that Daniel Stirling Senior, his grandfather, was indeed attempting to force his grandchildren to work on the ranch, together, for three years. Why else would anyone threaten to leave everything to a sworn enemy?

The other part of his brain was dealing with the monumental realization that he'd just inherited one fifth of a fortune. He could pay off Mikey. Get his car out of George's garage. All his financial worries were solvable now.

But there was more than that. There was Emma and Lizzie, too. He would be able to take care of them now. He could be a real father. He could—

"May I finish?" Watney bellowed over the din.

To their credit, the Stirling clan settled down, though Luke still glared in Danny's direction.

"Thank you." His jowls quivered a tad.

Luke interrupted before the older man could continue. "Let's focus on the ridiculous requirement that we work the ranch for three years." A red flush rose on his cheeks. He glared at Watney. "Isn't there some legal precedent here?"

"Yes." Watney speared him with a somber glance. "Your grandfather stated the terms of his will. You either comply or you don't."

Luke paled, making his scar more pronounced. "This is blackmail," he said.

Watney sighed. "I was your grandfather's lawyer for over thirty years. I knew the man as well as you did. Are any of you really surprised?" When no one responded, the lawyer continued. "The fact of the matter is, these are his wishes. Why don't you all take a few days to process this, and then we can meet again?"

It was pretty clear that Watney understood this was a lot for them to take in, let alone getting acquainted with their new half sibling. He collected his copious papers and left them alone in the room, nodding to the group as he shut the door.

A fresh and febrile awkwardness descended. At least, on Danny. Because everyone else—other than Dorthea—turned their attention to him.

"So," Luke said—rather pointedly, Danny thought. "What are *you* going to do?"

Danny blinked. "I—I don't know. I'm as surprised as all of you." Honestly, he'd expected much less. Little to nothing, to be precise. He needed time to work through all of this. Time without these people staring at him. Thank God, Lizzie had stayed. He'd never needed to talk to her more.

"I think we should head back to the house," DJ said. "We have a lot to discuss and I'd prefer to be somewhere private."

Everyone nodded and they all stood. As Luke gave a hand to Dorthea, he pinned Danny with a dark, incomprehensible look. "You, too, *brother*," he said on a hiss.

Oh? Oh, really? Now that they needed him? For their inheritance? Too bad. As low as his bank account might be, he had other priorities.

"Sorry," Danny said as nonchalantly as he could.

"But I can't stay." He glanced at his watch, just to make a point, even though he wasn't wearing one.

Sam's eyes widened. "Are you kidding? Where else could you possibly need to be right now?"

Danny's annoyance mingled with a strange sense of satisfaction as he took in their affronted expressions. Was it wrong that he kind of enjoyed irritating his...siblings?

He turned to DJ. "If you want to talk about this with me, it will have to be later."

DJ gave him a stern look, but nodded. "Will you come over for supper?"

Danny frowned. "I suppose."

"Great." Mark wrapped an arm around his shoulder. "I'll pick you up at the hotel around five. Will that work?"

"Yeah." He couldn't be standoffish to Mark, who was the only one who seemed to be making an effort at any sort of friendship. "All right." He nodded to all of them and skedaddled as fast as he could.

He was new to this whole sibling thing, but he'd learned one thing right off the bat. Family was best taken in small doses.

Chapter Five

Danny was still a little dumbfounded when he walked into the B&G after the meeting with his family. It took him a minute to find Lizzie waiting for him in a booth. When she saw him, she waved.

"So how did it go?" she asked as he slid into the booth. She passed her coffee to him and he took a long sip.

"Thanks." He slid the mug back. "Wow. It was something."

"So you do have a family?" Her eyes were bright, beautiful and slightly amused. He could tell she was dying to know. She probably thought it would be wonderful for him to finally have a real family. Yeah. He'd thought the same thing. Until he'd met them.

"I suppose." He let out something that was almost a laugh. "I'll probably have to take a blood test for that, too, but the blood test for Emma comes first. I promise."

Lizzie's smile faded into a glower. "Did they ask you for a blood test? Seems a little harsh for a first meeting. You'd think they might want to at least get to know you before asking for bodily fluids." Even after everything they'd been through together, she was loyal to a fault.

His mother was probably right: he didn't deserve her.

He set his hand on hers to calm her, at least a little. "Well, the lawyer said the blood test doesn't matter. He said I was specifically named in the will. Besides, I don't mind giving them their blood test, if they want it."

"So who asked for it?"

"One of my half brothers."

"What a jerk."

Danny shrugged. "I get it. I'm just some random yahoo, named in their grandfather's will."

"Are you going to do it?"

"Yes." He grinned at her frown. "But for my own peace of mind. It would feel wrong taking anything from them if I weren't really related."

"So…" She blew out a sigh. "What did you inherit? The grandfather clock you were wanting?"

He smiled at her joke, but shook his head. "It's a lot more than that. But there's a problem that comes with the inheritance."

Lizzie frowned. "What is it?"

"In order for any of us to inherit, we all have to work the ranch for three years. *I* have to work the ranch for three years."

"Is that a problem?"

"Hell, yes." His brow furrowed. "I don't want to be here when Emma's in Seattle. I want to be there, for her, no matter what."

"They can't *make* you live here." Her eyes widened in shock. "Can they?"

He shook his head. "If I flake, if anyone flakes, the entire family fortune goes to, apparently, the competition."

She gaped at him. "You're kidding. Who writes a will like this?"

His snort was dry. "One of *my* relatives, apparently."

"So you're torn between helping Emma and working the ranch."

"Pretty much."

She sat for a minute, thinking this through, and then she smiled at him. "Well, I don't see why you have to choose one or the other. I mean, you can work on the ranch and still see Emma. We're only a few hours away. Just like you said yesterday, you are not alone anymore. I'm in this with you. We'll make it work. For Emma."

His sigh, heavy though it was, lightened his soul. She was right. The two commitments were not exclusive. He *could* do it all.

"And," she said with a mischievous grin he remembered so well, "if your brother is a jerk, I'll defend you."

His chuckle was brusque. "He's pretty intimidating."

"I don't care." Damn, she was the best. Just the best friend ever.

Except he wanted much more than friendship from Lizzie. He always had.

It was the hardest damn thing Danny Diem had ever done, watching Lizzie get into her car that afternoon and, with a cheerful wave, leave him. Watching her leave was never easy, but it was different this time, because this time he was going to see her again soon. They were *connected* again. And connected by a bond that could never be broken. A child. Their child.

She'd sent pictures of Emma to his phone—glorious images of moments in her life he'd missed. But he still loved looking at them. Every glance made his heart swell more. All he wanted was to go to Seattle and meet his daughter. Maybe give her a hug if she wasn't too shy.

Was she shy? Lizzie hadn't said.

Suddenly his mind flooded with questions, all with no answers. What kind of cake did she like?

Was she a chocolate or strawberry fan? What size shoe did she wear? What did her voice sound like? What was her favorite toy?

Did she *want* a father?

That was the big question, wasn't it?

Well, he only had to wait a couple of days to find out everything. First, he had to face his family again.

As promised, Mark showed up at the hotel at five. The drive to the ranch didn't take long. As they passed through the massive gates, and then past endless fields, Danny found himself speechless at the scope of the place. But the house was even grander. He stared at it as Mark pulled up the drive.

"Wow."

It was all he could manage as he gazed at the sprawling three-story lodge-like ranch house. Beyond that, the property included several large barns, work sheds, a bunkhouse and a sprinkling of cabins.

Mark chuckled. "Yeah. Granddad must have thought he was going to have a large family who would always live here when he built it. Most of the rooms are empty, though. Only Sam, DJ and Grandma really live here. We were hoping that Luke would move back now that…" He trailed off and cleared his throat. "Now that he's no longer in the Marines."

Ah. That might explain the scars. And the limp. Danny didn't pry any further, but asked, "Don't you live here?"

Another chuckle. "Hell, no. I have my own place." He pointed to one of the cabins. "It's still on the property, but far enough away that the barking doesn't bother Grandma."

"The barking?"

"Yeah. I kind of have a lot of dogs." And, at Danny's curious glance, he explained, "I foster homeless pups. Aside from that, I like my privacy." This he said with a wink. He pulled up by the portico and put the truck in Park. "Come on. I'll give you the five-cent tour of the big house."

The foyer of the Stirling home was every bit as grand as its exterior, with polished wood floors that ran the length of the house, a magnificent curving staircase and a crystal chandelier holding a place of prominence above.

Apparently, beef ranching in Washington was a prosperous thing.

A slender young woman wearing an apron came out of the kitchen to greet them.

"Hey, Maria! Come meet Danny Diem. He'll be staying here awhile."

She nodded and offered a smile that made clear she'd noticed the family resemblance, as well, but she had the good grace not to gape. "Welcome, Danny."

Mark turned to him. "Maria helps take care of things around here. She's been with us for so long, she's practically part of the family."

Maria chuckled and blushed, but it was clear she was pleased.

"She's also helping out making meals because DJ scared away the cook."

"I did not scare him away," DJ boomed from the entryway.

Danny started because he hadn't heard him enter.

"You can be a little overbearing," Mark said.

"I am not overbearing," DJ snapped. And then, with no preface whatsoever, he turned to Danny and clipped, "Can I see you in my office. Now." Though it was framed as a request, it was anything but.

Danny took a deep breath as a tangle of frustration and resentment rushed through him. Who was DJ to boss him around?

"You'd better go," Mark suggested. "Trust me. It's easier in the long run."

Danny snorted. The way he saw it, these Stirlings needed him more than he needed them. Especially now that he was one-fifth owner of…everything.

The prospect overwhelmed him. He'd never owned anything worth more than his 'Vette, which wasn't saying much. The thought of having a piece of this incredible property… Well, it boggled his mind.

The fact that they needed him was particularly helpful, though, as it gave him the motivation to saunter after DJ, as though a private chat was no big deal.

But in truth, his gut was tight and there was a sour taste in his mouth. He wasn't looking forward to this in the slightest.

The office was a large room dominated by an antique desk scattered with papers and piled with files. A credenza by the door sported a collection of expensive-looking bronze statues. One wall had bookshelves that reached to the ceiling, and there was a small sitting area before a stone fireplace.

Naturally, DJ did not opt for the less formal venue. He took a seat behind the desk and waved at a chair across from him. This was a classic power play, and it just riled Danny further. He had to take a moment to compose himself before he sat. Or maybe he hesitated because he could tell it irked DJ. Hard to say.

A photograph on the credenza caught his attention. He had to pick it up. Had to stare.

"Yeah," DJ said. "That's my...*our* dad." A handsome man, tall, lean, standing by a fence, with a huge grin on his face. It was eerie how familiar he seemed. "He must have been, what, about thirty-two in that photo? Right before he died."

"How'd he pass?" The words came out hard and sharp, all of their own accord.

"Car accident."

"That must have been hard."

"Yeah." DJ's expression softened, but only for a second. And then, as though he'd reminded himself of his purpose, he became stern once more. "Sit. Please."

Once Danny was settled, DJ steepled his fingers and stared at him over them. "So," he said.

"So." Yeah. His older brother's manner was a little annoying.

DJ leaned forward, spearing Danny with his sharp gaze. "You're my father's…son."

His pause was long enough for Danny to fill in the blank. Irritation pricked at him. It appeared he wasn't the only bastard in the room. He inspected his fingernails. "So everyone tells me."

DJ ran a hand through his hair. "It's uncanny how much you are like him. Not just your looks. Your mannerisms, too."

"I wouldn't know. Considering I never met the man." It was hard to keep the bitterness from his tone—because, frankly, the *man* had never wanted to meet him—so he didn't bother.

DJ's jaw tightened. "Yet here you are to collect your inheritance."

"Look, I had no idea what that will said. I never wanted any part of your stupid ranch."

"Then why did you come?"

He could only tell the truth. "I came because I was curious."

"And because you need money?" There was something too knowing in DJ's gaze. It made acid churn in Danny's gut.

Did he need money? Yes. But he'd be damned

if he was going to beg for it. "Did I ask for your money? Did I ask for anything?" Danny crossed his arms over his chest. To hell with this guy.

When DJ realized Danny wasn't going to answer, he picked up a paper and perused it for a long while. When he spoke, it sent a curl of apprehension through Danny's gut. "Mikey Gerardo. Does that name ring a bell?"

A couple of them. Danny shifted in his seat. How had DJ found out about that?

"He is, in fact, a Vegas loan shark. Is he not?"

Danny narrowed his eyes, but didn't respond. What was the point?

"And you owe him nearly ten grand." DJ dropped the paper and fixed his gaze on Danny. "You need to know, right here and now, I don't just hand out stacks of money to strangers."

Fury rose in him. "Well, I don't take handouts—from anyone, DJ Stirling. And I never have."

"But surely you can see why I'm concerned? I don't want to bring that element into our lives."

Outrage and an unfamiliar kind of pain stabbed at his chest. DJ didn't even know him, and he was already rejecting him. "*That* element?" he hissed.

"How do you get so deeply in debt to a loan shark if you're not a compulsive gambler?" Was that a smirk on his face?

Danny set his jaw and glared at DJ. He wasn't going to explain himself to this privileged cowboy who'd never had to scrape and finagle to survive.

"I don't want anything from you. Or your siblings." Even to his own ears, he sounded petulant, but he really didn't know what else to say.

DJ stared at him for a minute. "Well, too bad about that, because we're in this together now."

"What the hell—"

"I'm not going to give you the money to pay off Gerardo." *Huge surprise*. But then, DJ *did* surprise him when he added, "But I will let you work for the money."

Danny snorted a laugh. "Work for…my own inheritance? Gee, thanks."

DJ slashed at the air with his hand. "I'm not talking about the will. I'm talking about the ten grand you need to pay off this loan shark. If you work the ranch for three months—and I mean work—I'll give you the ten grand."

"Three months?" He could do that. Couldn't he? "So then you would give me the money I need to pay off Mikey free and clear—"

DJ's lip curled into a grin. "I think I made it plain you'd be earning it. And trust me. You will be."

"Right. But… Other than that, no strings?"

The man's expression tightened, but he shook his head. "No."

Danny eyed him warily. Suspicion rippled through him. This just didn't add up. Why would DJ take the chance? Why would he give Danny what he needed and leave him free to ride off into the sunset in three months' time, even if it meant that the others would lose everything? How did that make any sense? There had to be some kind of angle here. There always was. "I guess I just don't understand why you'd do that for me."

DJ leaned back in his chair and huffed a breath. "All right. If I'm being perfectly honest, I'm hoping you decide to stay."

"Because of the inheritance." Yeah. That made sense.

"Sure. But also because I think it's what the old man wanted. For us all to try to be a family. Obviously he knew about you—no one else did, by the way. It probably stuck in his craw to have a Stirling out in the world somewhere, unrecognized as such. So, in the spirit of my grandfather's pride in the Stirling lineage, I'd like to put you on the payroll, just like everyone else. With full benefits."

Benefits. His pulse thrummed. "Including medical?"

"Yup."

Wow. That could come in handy now. For Emma.

But no one had ever given Danny anything. And as much as he wanted to believe, he distrusted it.

His expression must have telegraphed as much because DJ sighed and raked back his hair. "Look, Danny. Like it or not, blood test or not, it's pretty clear you're my father's son. Our brother. And Stirlings take care of their own."

Danny gaped at him.

Stirlings take care of their own.

The phrase made his throat hurt. He'd never been *included* like this, not ever. It was something shiny and new for him. Something a little frightening, too.

He couldn't deny how deeply DJ's gesture touched him, despite his gruffness. He couldn't admit it, either.

His brother stood, rounded the desk and thrust out a large hand. "Deal?" His expression was hard and unyielding, but Danny sensed the hope behind it. He hated to quash it.

He stood, as well, and faced DJ. "I… There's something else."

DJ's hand slowly dropped. A muscle ticked in his cheek. "What is it?"

"I—I have a daughter."

His brother nodded. "She's welcome to live here, too."

Danny shook his head and sucked in a deep breath. "It's not that. She's…sick."

"Sick?"

"She has something called aplastic anemia. She desperately needs a bone-marrow transplant. I'm heading to Seattle tomorrow to be tested at Children's Hospital, to see if I'm a match. That… That was the other meeting I had today. With her mother."

DJ's eyebrows furrowed, as though he didn't completely buy this story, so Danny pulled out his phone and showed him a picture of Emma. Even as he saw it again, his heart hitched. "This is her. This is Emma."

DJ's Adam's apple worked as he stared at the picture. "She's…beautiful."

"She's very sick." As his brother's expression wavered, he added, "Look, DJ. I'm more than happy to work this ranch for three months, three years, whatever. But I need to take care of my daughter first. I *have* to go to Seattle. But I promise, I'll come back. Do all the things we talked about. I just need to take care of her first."

After a long moment, DJ nodded. "All right. You go take care of your daughter. Once she's better, you'll live here, work here, for three years, just like the will requires. And if Emma needs anything that we can provide, you let me know. Deal?" He held out his hand again.

Danny stared at DJ, his heart filled with another unfamiliar emotion. This one was harder to name, but it definitely made his chest ache.

As he took his brother's warm and callused hand, it occurred to him that this family thing might not be so disagreeable after all.

As soon as Lizzie awoke on Monday morning, she showered and then headed straight to the hospital to pick up Emma, who had fought off her infection and was cleared to come home. It took some effort to convince Nan to go to work instead of coming along. After all, she'd been with her sister every step of the way since Emma's birth. But when Lizzie told her she needed time alone with Emma to talk about what had transpired with Danny, Nan understood.

As difficult and as awkward as the conversation promised to be, it had to be had. Perhaps banana splits might help?

Unfortunately, Emma was too smart to be fooled.

Once they got home and Lizzie started pulling out all the necessary ingredients—including sprinkles—Emma looked up at her, over the ubiquitous Minnie Mouse mask, and sighed.

"Honey. What's wrong?"

"Banana splits? Again?"

Lizzie nearly choked. "What? I thought you loved banana splits. Look. Sprinkles."

"I do. But Mommy, the last time you made banana splits, it was 'cause they needed to give me those awful shots. And the time before that it was the icky-picc." She touched her PICC line, the central catheter they'd inserted for her treatments and occasionally to aid with liquid nutrition when she was particularly ill. "And before that—"

"All right. Okay." So it was confirmed. She was a coward who ruthlessly used helpless banana splits to soften blows. "Let's sit on the sofa, shall we?"

Emma nodded and made her way into the living room as though on the way to her doom. Lizzie sat beside her and took her hand.

Her daughter met her gaze with those beautiful brown eyes, wide and glistening with tears. "How bad is it?" she asked through a quivering mask.

The question broke Lizzie's heart. For one thing, after everything she'd been through, her daughter now *expected* bad news. For another, Lizzie wasn't sure how bad it really was. Emma would meet her father, a man who'd never wanted a family, but now seemed resolved to it. In fact, he'd seemed excited about meeting her.

But it was Lizzie's job to protect her child. The last thing she wanted to do was set her up for disappointment. If she told Emma she might have found a potential donor, and then Danny wasn't a match, well, that would be more than a disappointment. It would be a disaster.

Somehow, telling her that Danny was her father seemed like less of a risk. As nerve-racking as that thought was.

Through tangled emotions, Lizzie had to admit that she wasn't sure if she was more frightened of Emma's heartbreak, or her own.

She tamped down her fears and sucked in a deep breath. "You know I went away for a few days."

"Yes. Where did you go?"

"I went to a little town called Butterscotch Ridge."

Emma's eyes crinkled. "I like butterscotch."

"It's a little town in eastern Washington. Over the mountains. Here. Look." She pulled out her phone's map. "We're here, in Seattle. I went here."

Her daughter glanced at the map, then took

Lizzie's hand and inspected her nail polish. "Why did you go there?"

"I, um…" This was harder than she'd imagined. Might as well just blurt it out. "I went to find your father." There. She'd said it. She looked at Emma and swallowed heavily.

How she wished her daughter didn't need to wear that blasted mask. It would be nice, at this moment, to be able to gauge her whole expression, not just the eyes.

Emma stilled. Stared at her. "The sperm donor?"

"Ah, yes." Lizzie swallowed an incongruous laugh. "He doesn't like that title."

"So you found him?" Her daughter's voice was hushed, tight.

"I did."

"And… Does he want to meet me?"

Lizzie took a shuddering breath. Of course, *that* was the question swirling in her tiny little head.

"Yes. He wants to meet you. Why wouldn't he? You're perfect."

"No, I'm not. Did you tell him I'm sick?" Emma leaped to her feet and began to pace. "What if he doesn't want a sick daughter? What if I'm not good enough for him to stay? What if—?"

"Oh, sweetie." Lizzie caught Emma and pulled her into a tight hug. "He knows you're sick. He wants to help."

Emma's brow rumpled. "How can he help? Is he a doctor?"

"No. No. Not a doctor. But he has agreed to get a bone-marrow test. You know. To see if he can give you healthy cells for your body to grow."

Emma plopped back down on the sofa. "So," she said after a moment. "I have a dad. A real dad?"

"Yes." Lizzie took her hand. "You do."

"What's his name?"

"Danny."

"Danny." Emma tasted the word. "What do I call him, though?"

What would she call him? Lizzie had no clue. This was all uncharted territory. "Perhaps you can ask him that when he comes to see you."

Emma's head whipped around. "He's coming?" she asked in a squeal that only five-year-old ears could tolerate. No doubt all the dogs in Seattle started howling inexplicably. "He's coming here?" She leaped up and danced around, and then checked her reflection in the glass. "Oh, my gosh. What will I wear? Does he like Minnie Mouse? I have to clean my room." She dropped back onto the sofa and stared at Lizzie with an intensity that reminded her of how Emma had been...before she got sick. "When? When will he be here?"

Oh, dear. Her daughter was...excited. Lizzie wasn't sure if she should be relieved or terrified. Nothing disappointed like expectation. Especially when it came to men. At least, that was her experience. "He'll be here tomorrow." *Tomorrow.* Goodness. The time had flown by.

"Tomorrow?" That squeal again. "We need to hurry." She grabbed Lizzie's hand and towed her toward the bedrooms. "We need to get ready. Everything has to be perfect."

"Perfect?"

"Yes." Emma leveled a too-serious look on Lizzie. "We need to make sure my daddy loves me."

Her gut clenched. How on earth did she respond to that? "Of course, he loves you." Who wouldn't love her?

But she couldn't silence the questions that plagued her. Sure, her interaction with Danny had seemed to go well. He'd seemed to be excited about meeting Emma. But this was real life. This was *scary* real life.

Who knew how long he'd stay? Once he realized how hard life with a sick child could be?

How long would it be before he left them?

How long would it be until he broke both their hearts?

Danny made the drive to Seattle on Tuesday in a blur. He barely noticed the change of scenery as he left the eastern desert and drove into the mountain passes, and then into the cool, lush green forests of western Washington. He did notice the rain, though. It hit as he passed North Bend and continued all the way to Seattle.

The weather seemed to mirror his anxiety, which grew with each passing mile marker, reminding him that he was coming closer and closer to his destination, to his daughter and Lizzie.

He worried whether Emma would accept him, to be sure, but thoughts of Lizzie bubbled deep, as well.

Memories of their time together taunted him.

He remembered her touch. Her kiss. The sweet smell of her as she slept in his arms. He had ached for her, for years, though he'd worked hard to convince himself he didn't care. And now?

He couldn't wait to see her again. And he was terrified at the same time. Because that longing was tinged with frustration and hurt that she'd kept the truth from him about their daughter for five long years—time that he longed to make up…if he was lucky enough to get a second chance.

Before he knew it, his GPS directed him into the parking garage of her building. The tall modern structure that seemed to be made of glass faced Elliott Bay.

After he found a parking spot, he took a minute to sanitize his hands and pull on a mask—because everything he'd read made clear any exposure to germs could make Emma ill. Then he headed to the elevator. It was thickly carpeted, with mirrored walls. He tried not to look at himself as he glided to the tenth floor, but then, at the last minute, he realized he should check his reflection. Indeed, he had a rooster tail, which he hurriedly smoothed down.

The walk from the elevator to Lizzie's condo

seemed to take forever. And then, once he arrived, he sucked in a deep breath before he knocked.

This was it. This was the moment he would meet his daughter. Finally.

His heart stopped as Lizzie opened the door. She was so beautiful, he just wanted to stand there and take her in for a moment. As he languished in that momentary daze, and with no preamble, she gave each of his hands a squirt of Purell.

"What are you doing?" he asked.

"Emma has a low tolerance for germs. We try to keep her exposure at a minimum."

"I know that. I sanitized in the car."

"Did you push the buttons in the elevator?" she asked brusquely.

Heat rose on his cheeks. To cover it up, he rubbed his hands together, trying to make sure the gel was thoroughly absorbed. "Nice place," he said after a quick glance around. The apartment was sleek and roomy, and had a nice view. It was also spotless.

"Thanks. It's Nan's condo." She crossed into the kitchen to set the sanitizer on the counter. He hated that her tone was so casual. As though he was just dropping by for coffee or something. They'd lived together for several years. They'd been intimate. They'd been a couple. Now they were…strangers. He hated it.

"You're living with Nan?" Though he'd heard about her, they'd never met.

"Mmm-hmm. We've all lived here, well, since I left Vegas."

"It's nice." Damn. He'd already said that.

"There's three bedrooms. Emma and I are over here." She pointed to the right. "Nan's in the master." To the left, apparently.

"It's so…clean."

"We keep it tidy. For Emma." A reminder, on a deeper level, that Emma was different. "How was your drive?"

He shrugged. "It rained once I crossed the mountains."

She gave a little laugh. "That does happen."

"Since my car broke down, my brother Mark let me borrow his truck." He glanced around the sterile condo. "Um, is Emma here?"

"She's with Nan, getting an infusion. They'll be here soon. I thought you and I could talk privately first. You know, set some boundaries."

His mood took a nosedive. He didn't like the boundaries idea at all, but he nodded. He wanted—no, needed—to make this easy for her, even if it cost him. "All right."

"Shall we sit?" She waved at the sofa and he complied, though it felt wrong, sitting there on her sofa as she took a seat on the other side of the coffee table. Too far away, he thought, for the conversation they were to have.

He shoved that thought from his mind and laced his fingers together, trying to think of something to say. He wasn't sure why it was so difficult now, when back in Butterscotch Ridge, they'd been chattering like magpies.

"So," he finally said. "You said something about boundaries?"

"Oh. Um. Yes." She brushed back her auburn hair and he watched it fall over her shoulders. God, she was pretty, even though she wore a mask, even though there were worry lines on her forehead and her eyes crinkled when she smiled. How he wished she would smile now. "Not restrictions, per se. I just wanted to ask you to…"

When she hesitated, he prompted her. "Yes?"

"I just… Oh, how do I say this? Could you please…take it slow with her?"

Take it slow? What the hell did that mean? Was Lizzie expecting him to act like a random stranger, some…*sperm donor*, when he met his own daughter? He didn't really understand the anger building in him, but he recognized the feeling of being sidelined.

"Does she even know I'm her…father?" He didn't know why the word caught in his throat.

She nodded, and he nearly collapsed in relief. "I've told her. And that you're planning to be tested." Her eyes narrowed. "You are still planning to do that, aren't you?"

"Of course. I've already made an appointment. Tomorrow, in fact."

She lurched back and gaped at him as though he'd sprouted a third eye. "You have?"

The incredulity in her tone slayed him. "I said I would. Did you think I would flake?" But even as he asked, he knew. He knew, because flaking was what the old Danny did best. But that was why he was here—to prove to her that everything was different. That *he* was different. "I have changed, you know."

"I know. I know. I... Thank you, Danny. I can't tell you how much I appreciate this."

His blood froze. "Let's get something straight. I'm not doing you a favor. She's my daughter, too. And I care about what happens to her."

A flush rose on her cheeks, but before she had a chance to retort—thank God, because this was not going well—they heard the sound of the key in the lock. The clicks filled the room like a live wire. Danny's blood fizzled and his back went ramrod-straight. His attention whipped to the door, and he stared, breathless and terrified and hopeful all at once.

The door swung open and Emma appeared. His gaze locked on her. He had the impression of a small sprite with a tumble of black curls that looked just like the ones he'd had as a kid. She wore a mask decorated with mice wearing colorful hair bows. It bothered Danny that the mask covered most of her face. Only her eyes were visible, and they were wide and pinned on him.

"Come on in, Emma," Lizzie said when she seemed to hesitate.

"Go ahead, sweetie," the woman behind her encouraged. She had to be Lizzie's sister. They looked alike, except for the color of their hair.

"Danny," Nan said with a curt nod, then she headed straight to her bedroom to give them privacy, which was decent of her. Because who knew how this would go?

Emma stepped toward him. When she came close, she tipped her head and studied him from one angle and then another.

His pulse pounded. His lungs burned. She was perfect. Perfect. He longed to sweep her up into his arms and hug her, but he knew it was far too soon for such a gesture. He was a stranger to her. And he didn't want to frighten her. Aside from that, she was sick. And yeah, she was pale and far too frail for the hungry hug he wanted to give her.

"Hi," he said, even though he knew such a greeting was utterly absurd and wholly inadequate for the circumstance of such a meeting.

She tipped her head again and her eyes narrowed. "So you're my daddy," she said in a matter-of-fact, far too grown-up voice.

He cleared his throat in an attempt to swallow a sudden knot. "I, ah, am. How do you…feel about that?"

Her tiny shoulder lifted. Then she said, "I want to see your face."

Oh, hell. Of course she did. Not knowing the protocol here, he glanced at Lizzie, who nodded subtly. Danny sucked in a deep breath and pulled down his mask. He let her study him as long as he could hold his breath, then he raised the mask again and gasped for air.

She seemed impressed. At least he imagined she did. And then she said, "If you're my daddy, where have you been?"

And, yeah, his heart clenched.

Lizzie, to her credit, leaned forward and said, "Remember? We talked about this. He didn't know about you, honey."

Emma's attention never left his face. "Why did you leave us?"

He cleared his throat. "I didn't, not exactly." When Emma's probing gaze sharpened, he quickly added, "I wasn't ready to be a good dad. I guess I needed time to learn how to do the job right."

Emma considered this for a moment and then asked, "Well? Are you ready now?"

Hell. Was he? He decided on the truth. "I want to be ready." *God, did he!* "But I don't know anything about being a parent." He stared into her eyes. "Would you be willing to...teach me?"

Those eyes, so like his own, widened. He wished he could see more of her face, but the mask obstructed most of it. A sly crinkle at the corners of her eyes gave him a clue to her thoughts, though. "Are you a fast learner?" she asked.

He blinked. "Um, well, sure."

"Do you like ice cream?"

"Ice cream? I'm all for it." Hey, maybe this would be easier than he thought.

"Every day?"

He gulped. "Well…" He glanced at Lizzie, but she was just watching. Possibly biting her cheek to keep from laughing. No help there. "I like it a lot, but I don't think I would want to eat it every day."

Emma's gaze narrowed until her lashes nearly fanned her cheeks. "We'll have to work on that."

And he couldn't help it. He threw back his head and laughed. At that moment, he knew beyond a shadow of a doubt that he was utterly, head-over-heels in love with his daughter.

Chapter Six

Danny stayed and had dinner with them that night at Emma's insistence.

Emma also insisted on pizza, which wasn't a treat Lizzie allowed very often because Emma's foods needed to be nutrient dense. But, as Emma proclaimed, this was a special occasion. Lizzie found she unexpectedly enjoyed Danny's presence in the family circle. She especially enjoyed his awkwardness with this new role. It was fun watching the confident man she remembered stumble to find answers to Emma's unending questions.

Yes, it was awkward at first, but as they warmed up to each other from six feet apart—specifically as Nan warmed up to Danny and set aside her veil of distrust—the meal became more comfortable. Even fun.

It was a lot more difficult for Lizzie to watch Emma and Danny bonding. Not because it wasn't a beautiful thing. It was. But it reminded her of just how much he'd missed. And whose fault it was.

The guilt forced her into silence.

Fortunately, those two didn't need anyone else to share an animated conversation, which, at this moment, centered on the probability that unicorns could have evolved from horses. It was adorable to watch, but painful, too. It was clear Emma adored her father. And it was clear he already felt the same.

She wasn't losing Emma, she reminded herself, even though, on some level, it felt that way. If anything, this change would enrich their lives and possibly save Emma from a lot of pain. But that was hard to hold on to as her limbic brain went into protective overdrive.

And then, there was the other concern, the one bubbling at the back of her brain ever since she'd seen Danny again at the B&G and her body had sparked at his nearness.

It had been five years since she'd even *thought* about…sex.

And now, here she was, sitting across the table from the one man who could destroy her composure and resolve, the man who could dissolve all her carefully erected barriers. A glance from him made her heart hitch. His smile made something deep in her belly tingle. His laugh made her limbs warm and loose. At one point, he caught her eye and a zing of excitement careened through her.

Naturally, she looked away. No one should feel this kind of lust at the dinner table with a child in attendance.

"So your appointment is tomorrow?" she blurted.

He nodded. "Ten a.m."

"And where are you staying?" Nan asked.

Danny blinked. "Well, I...figured I'd find a motel or something."

Emma's expression turned pleading. "Can't he stay here?" She turned to Lizzie with hands clasped. "Please? Please, please, please?"

Lizzie glanced at Nan, but her sister was no help at all. "It does make sense, I guess," she said with a shrug.

Great. She was outnumbered. She forced a smile, against all her better instincts. "Of course, you can stay here. That is, if you don't mind sleeping on the couch."

"Yay!" Emma bounced up and down on her seat. "The couch is a bed, too. It opens up into a bed!" she said, as though this was the most novel idea ever. "Say you'll stay. You can even read me a story. I *always* get a story before bed."

Lizzie blinked. Storytime was *her* thing.

But before she got too put out, Danny noticed Lizzie's expression and said, "Only if your mom says it's okay."

That did help ease her angst. A little.

His wink, however, didn't help quash the heat in her belly much at all.

After Emma's bath, Lizzie got her daughter into her pj's, then snuggled into her bed with her favorite book. But Emma wouldn't let Lizzie start until Danny came to snuggle on her other side. "We're a sandwich," Emma said with a giggle. "A family sandwich."

Danny and Lizzie glanced at each other over her head, and Lizzie tried to ignore the warmth swelling in her chest. Tried to ignore all the fantasies she'd had, once upon a time, where she and Danny were together, with Emma nestled between them.

It was too poignant for words.

But Emma wasn't interested in her mother's melodrama. "Read," she commanded, squishing herself deeper between them.

Lizzie did as she was told, although she did have to let Danny read every other page, because Emma insisted.

When the story was finished, Emma wanted another one, but Lizzie was too wise to her ways to comply. "One story," she reminded her daughter, who made a face. Apparently, she'd thought, now that her daddy was here, all the rules would fly out the window. "Besides, Danny has a big day tomorrow. He has to go to the hospital."

"But we're going with him," Emma said. "Just like you always take me when I have tests, Mommy."

Oh, Lord. How to respond to such logic? "I'll call Dr. Blake tomorrow and ask if we can come too. Okay?"

Emma bounced up and down and cried, "Hurrah!"

"Thank you," Danny said, eyeing Lizzie's hesitant expression.

"Don't worry," said Emma. "If you like, when we're there, you can hold my hand."

Danny hid a smile. "I can?"

Emma nodded. "It makes it better when someone holds your hand."

It was such a solemn offering, it made Lizzie want to cry. Emma had been through too much at her age, and it bruised her heart to see how keenly her daughter understood others' pain—but it also made her proud. Holding back her emotions, she gave her daughter a kiss and slipped from the bed. "Sleep well, Emma."

"You, too, Mommy." She reached to Danny for a kiss, as well. "Good night… Daddy."

A flush rose on his cheeks. He only hesitated for a second before he gave her a long hug and a quick peck on the forehead through his mask, as though he was trying something new for the first time. "I'm…" He cleared his throat. "I'm so happy to know you, Emma."

Her eyes glinted. "I'm so happy you are here with me, too."

Together, Lizzie and Danny made their way into the hall, but he glanced back for one more look before she shut off the light. As though he couldn't get enough of Emma.

He removed his mask as they stepped into the living room, and so did she. Nan had retired for the night, so they were alone. He whirled around and stared at Lizzie. "She's perfect. Just perfect."

She nodded. It was all she could manage. She tried opening her mouth to respond, but nothing came out.

"Are you all right?" he asked.

"Yes. Yes. Of course. I am just so happy the two of you finally met."

A complete lie. Well, a partial lie. She was happy. It was a huge load off her conscience, but the old guilt still clung. It was her fault five years of Emma's life had passed without a father. It was her fault.

He stepped closer and reached out a thumb, dabbing at her lashes. "What are these? Tears?"

"No." She turned away, swiping at her cheeks.

"Please tell me what's wrong."

Her pulse thudded once. "I just… You missed so much—"

He stopped her with a finger over her lips. As she drew in a breath, his scent came along with it and made her head spin. "No," he said fiercely. "None of that. You did what you thought was best for Emma back then, and who am I to say you were wrong? I was a selfish son of a bitch."

"You weren't—"

"I *told* you I didn't want kids. And to be honest, I didn't." He barked a laugh and raked his fingers through his hair. "I wasn't ready to make that kind of commitment back then, and we both know it."

"Things might have been different if I'd told you about Emma that night."

He sighed. "Maybe. Maybe not. There's no point in going down that rabbit hole. Let's just focus on where we are now. I, for one, am happy to be here." He moved closer. "With Emma. With you. I've... missed you, Lizzie." His breath was warm on her cheek, fragrant.

"I've missed you, too." A whisper, because he was too close for her brain to work effectively. All she could think about was getting closer.

So when he pulled her into a hug, she went with it. Gloried in it. His arms enfolded her in a comfort and warmth she had ached for. His scent wrapped around her like a blanket. As the hug continued, his thumb stroked her back. Something so simple and innocent should never prompt the thoughts that sprouted in her head. But she couldn't help it. She couldn't help the growing desire to take his hand and lead him into her bedroom...

Which was right next to Emma's.

Her lustful thoughts faded instantly.

She pulled back, to shake her head, and say something about taking things slowly, about taking their time, but before she could, he touched his lips to hers. Just touched them, gently, sweetly.

She melted into him, lost. He made a satisfied noise and deepened the kiss. She met him halfway, her tongue touching his in a tentative invitation. His growl deepened. He turned his head to get a better angle…and froze.

Lizzie barely noticed. She was far too transfixed by the feel of his abs beneath his shirt and the heat pouring from him. He was just as hot as he'd been when—

"Ahem." Danny cleared his throat, and she frowned at him.

"What?" Okay, the word came out a little sharp, but she was annoyed by the interruption…from *him*!

He nodded toward the bedrooms. "We have an audience," he whispered.

Uh-oh. Heat swept through her, then she wrenched herself from Danny's hold and whirled around. Emma stood in the hallway avidly watching them. "What are you doing?" she asked with mild curiosity.

"Um…" Apparently, Danny still had the wherewithal to answer. "I was kissing your mom."

"Why?"

"Because… I, um, wanted to thank her for dinner?"

Emma's mask puffed as though she'd blown out a breath. "It's really gross-looking."

"Is it?" Danny asked through a laugh.

Lizzie had no idea why he was laughing. This was no laughing matter.

Emma crossed her little arms over her little chest. "Kissing is gross. Why do people do it?"

Danny grinned. "Well, Emma, there will come a day when you want to kiss a boy…" He trailed off as the prospect percolated in his brain.

Emma made a face. "And?"

"Uh, and don't do it."

"Not until you're married," Lizzie added. And when Danny gaped at her, because *they* certainly hadn't followed that rule, she gored him with her elbow.

"Uh, yeah. What your mother says."

"And your mother says it's way past your bedtime, young lady. Come on. Tomorrow is a big day." She took Emma's hand and led her back to bed before fetching clean sheets for Danny's sofa bed.

But she didn't kiss him again.

Still, it was doubtful she would get any sleep at all after that amazing blast from the past.

Danny didn't sleep well at all that night. And not just because the sofa bed was lumpy. There seemed to be a bar running vertically, right over his backbone. After tossing and turning for a bit, he finally found a comfortable position and just lay there, staring up at the ceiling. He tried not to obsess about how Lizzie wasn't very far away. Tried not to obsess on that kiss and how gratifying it had been. Tried not to convince himself she'd be welcoming, if he knocked.

He knew it was the wrong time for any of that, but he still couldn't evict the urge, or the desire whipping through him. It had, after all, been a long, long time for him.

He must have slept, because when he awoke, the room was lighter and there was a small figure standing by his side. Emma. Without her mask; it hung slack around her neck. He stared, soaking in her features.

She smiled at him. "Are you awake?" she asked.

"I am." He wriggled into a sitting position and glanced at his phone. Ugh. It was 5:30 a.m. "Shouldn't you be wearing your mask?" he asked.

She rolled her eyes and then pulled it on. He reached for his and did the same. "Are you scared?" she asked. "About the test?" Her expression radiated concern.

"A little."

At his admission, she hopped onto the bed next to him and took his hand in both of hers. "Don't be scared. It'll be okay."

He shivered when he thought how many times *she'd* heard those words, whispered over clasped hands. He squeezed her fingers. "How do you do this, sweetie?" he asked her. "All this medical stuff? Does it—does it scare you?"

Her chin wobbled a little. "Mommy says I'm very brave."

He wanted to hug her. He wanted to crush her to him with all his heart, but he didn't, because she was—above all things—fragile and precious. Instead, he gently looped her hair behind her ear. "You are very brave and now that I'm here, I want to be brave just like you. Would you show me how?"

"Yes." Her smile in her eyes said it all, until it faded. She peeped up at him, brows rumpled with concern. "Are you going to stay with us forever?" she asked. The question was an arrow in the heart.

"I—I want to. I really do." Why did life have to be so complicated all of a sudden? Oh. Right. Because he was a father. "Hey. I have a question for you. Do you like pancakes?"

She gave a squeal and bounced up and down on his sofa bed. "I love them."

"Good. Because that's the only thing I know how to make. You want some breakfast?"

In the end, Emma had to help him, because he had no idea where anything was. Together they made way too many pancakes and then sat and ate and talked about silly and profound things until Nan made an appearance. She stopped short, in her crisp business suit, and stared in horror at the kitchen countertops.

It was only then that Danny realized what a mess they'd made. There was batter everywhere. "Um, don't worry. We'll clean it up," he said immediately.

Emma giggled. "It's okay. Nan likes messes."

"And Nan likes pancakes, too," said Nan, putting two of the leftovers on a plate. "I see you found the blueberries," she teased her niece.

"Antioxi ants," Emma said in something of a cheer.

Nan shot him a grin. "You might want to clean this up before Lizzie wakes up, though. She's the neat freak."

"Thanks for the tip." He grinned back. It was surprising how well they were getting along, considering the circumstances. Though, on second thought, it shouldn't be. Nan was a lot like Lizzie, except that she wore suits and carried a briefcase and argued cases before judges.

"What do you want to be when you grow up, Emma?" he asked after Nan had left for work with a travel mug of coffee and a pancake neatly rolled up in her hand for the road.

Emma smiled—and he was pleased to see it. She'd taken off her mask to eat, but it dangled around her neck, never far away. As they had at dinner, they each sat at one end of the table, as far apart as possible. Small cost to keep his baby safe, he figured.

"I think I want to be a doctor," she said.

"A doctor!" He raised an eyebrow. "That sounds great."

"Yes." Her expression sobered as she set down her fork. "I want to make little kids better when they get sick."

"I see."

"Or a veterinarian. 'Cause I really like animals. Or maybe an astronaut."

"They all sound like great jobs."

"But I have to get better first. What do you do?" she asked. Right there, out of the blue.

He gulped. What on earth should he tell her? That he'd worked in security for casinos? That he once worked at a liquor store in downtown Vegas that got robbed on a regular basis? That he'd once had a gig as a DJ at a rave? He decided to focus on his new life, rather than his moldy old one. "Well, my family has a ranch and they've invited me to work there."

"Really?" Her eyes lit up. "Do they have animals?"

"They certainly do."

Emma did a little dance in her chair. "What kind?"

"Good morning."

Danny's head spun around at Lizzie's voice. As he caught sight of her, heat bubbled through him. Damn, she looked fresh in the morning.

Danny grinned at her. "Did you sleep well?"

She shot him a glare as she poured herself a cup of coffee. "'Bout as good as you, I suppose."

Well, there you go. Nice to know they'd both had a rough night.

"So, you were telling Emma about the ranch," Lizzie said, but he could tell she was more interested in changing the subject than any burning need to hear about the wide-open ranges of eastern Washington.

Unfortunately, Danny didn't know much. "They raise cows."

"Ooh." Emma nodded. "Cows are big."

"Yes. Yes, they are." This much he knew, at least.

"Do they have bunnies there?"

"Ah…" He blinked. "Not sure. Maybe?"

"'Cause I like bunnies. I always wanted a bunny, but Mommy says no. We live in the city. But bunnies are little enough to live in a condo. Don't you think?" This she asked with a spearing gaze. As though she fully expected Danny to overturn her mother's proclamation.

"Bunnies are small," he agreed, and when Lizzie narrowed her eyes at him, he added, "But I heard they can eat through plaster. Your mom might not like holes in the walls."

Emma's eyes widened. "Really?"

"Honey," Lizzie said gently. "You know why you can't have pets."

"But when I get better—"

The pain in Lizzie's eyes surprised him. In an epiphany that made his chest hurt, he realized *she* wasn't completely convinced Emma would get better. Not even now that he was here to help. It was a sobering revelation.

He longed to tell them both that he was going to be a perfect match. And Emma *would* get better. And he'd get her a bunny. Ten of them, maybe. Or two. Two would probably be enough. But he didn't *say* as much because he knew he had to honor Lizzie's concern. And not just because he wanted to make her happy, or because he wanted to be a partner to her in this. It was simply wrong to make promises to a child when you can't control the outcome.

Though he'd do everything in his power to control this one, and help where he could, because he couldn't imagine losing the daughter he'd only just met.

"It's about time to go," Lizzie said.

Emma's eyes widened. "Did Dr. Blake say I can come?" she asked.

Lizzie sighed. "He said yes. And he'll be there to see you, too. Isn't that nice?"

"Yes. Because he gets to meet my dad." Emma came to his side and took his hand.

Lizzie's lips tightened. "Emma, honey, if you're done eating, sanitize your hands and put on your mask."

Emma sighed heavily and complied. Danny hated seeing her face disappear again, but then she glanced at him and rolled her eyes in what she clearly felt was unified exasperation on the bunny topic, and he had to smile. "I take it Dr. Blake is your doctor?"

"Aunt Nan says he's hubba hubba," Emma said. "Is he?"

"Mmm-hmm. He thinks my mom is cute. He said so."

Oh, really? Handsome Dr. Blake had a thing for Lizzie? Something sour swirled among the pancakes in his gut. It didn't help that, when he glanced at Lizzie, she blushed.

Well, one thing was certain. He wasn't looking forward to meeting Dr. Blake. Not in the least.

As it turned out, Dr. Blake was way too good-looking. Danny didn't like him right away, even though he was professional and kind and greeted Danny warmly when they all met in his office. He greeted Lizzie warmly, too, which Danny found mildly irritating.

"I'm so glad you decided to be tested," the doctor said as they shook hands. It rankled almost as much as Lizzie's *appreciation* comment.

"She's *my* daughter," he said, holding the dude's hand just a smidgen longer than necessary. Okay. All right. He was a doctor. And, yes, he was doing his best to help Emma. But seriously. Would Lizzie even consider someone like this? He was…young. And *what* was with the hair gel?

This, of course, led to another, more disturbing question. He hadn't asked Lizzie if she had a boyfriend. Why hadn't he asked about that?

Dr. Blake grimaced and pulled back his hand. Flexed it. Then he clapped Danny on the back. "Of course, she's your daughter. I mean, look at you."

He gestured his clipboard toward Emma, who curtsied. Then he turned the clipboard on Danny. "Now, if you could look over the paperwork? I need your signature on some documents. And if you could fill out this medical history form, that would be great."

The form the doctor handed him was ridiculous. They wanted to know everything about him and his family history. All he could offer was that his mother had some painful disease called endometriosis. Beyond that, they wanted to know if he smoked, drank excessively, had AIDS or HIV, arthritis, asthma, lupus, spinal problems, hemophilia, history of blood clots, sleep apnea, depression, diabetes…and so much more. Relieved, he checked *no* on everything and signed with a wide scrawl.

"Great." Dr. Blake collected all the papers. "Let's go down to the lab, shall we?"

Danny nodded and forced a smile at Emma, but honestly, he was a little scared.

All right. He was terrified.

First of all, even though he'd done a little research of the process, he knew this could hurt, depending on what tests they ended up running after the initial cheek swab. But even that was an infinitesimal horror against the biggest risk of all. That his bone marrow might not match. That—after all this—they might still lose Emma.

But it would match, he reminded himself.

It had to.

A young nurse greeted them at the lab with a

wide smile. Or maybe her smile was for Dr. Blake. There might have been some fluttering lashes. "Well, hello," she said to the doctor, then she shot a smile at Emma, as well. "You're back to visit me, sweetie?"

"Not me," Emma said, waving in Danny's direction. "My daddy is getting tested."

His heart skipped a beat. She'd introduced him as her daddy. It made a warm glow fill his chest, which he thrust out proudly. "I'm her dad," he said. An unnecessary proclamation, but it felt damn good to say.

Dr. Blake handed over all his paperwork. "It's a good thing you're all prepared," the nurse said. "It'll save time. Come on through."

Unfortunately, this invitation was for Danny alone. He glanced back at Emma and made a face.

She patted his hand. "Don't worry. You'll do good."

He blew out a breath and followed the nurse down the hall into a tiny room bristling with far too many needles.

Once they were alone, she smiled at him. "So, do you know how this works?"

"A little."

"Well, the HLA test looks at genetic markers on your white blood cells. If the markers match Emma's, you may be eligible to serve as a donor." She smiled again. Far too perkily for the circumstances, he thought irritably. "The first step is a cheek swab."

He opened his mouth and held as still as he could. It was quicker than he figured it would be.

As the nurse tucked the swab in to a specimen bag, he sucked in a breath. "Okay. What's next?"

"We may do a follow-up blood draw to run additional tests if this one matches."

He shook his head. "So that was it?" That was all? That simple. Like, a second, or less. Amazing. This little swab could determine whether he could help save Emma's life.

"For today, yes. We'll send this to the lab and let you know in a couple weeks," she said, waggling the sample. "That's the standard, but hopefully it'll come in on the earlier side."

"Great. Thank you."

She nodded. "Sure. Anything for Emma. We just adore her. I hope she finds a match."

Danny headed back to the waiting room, musing at the ease of the first test, but stopped short in the hall when he saw the man exiting one of the other testing-room doors.

Because he knew this man.

He stared in shock. "Luke?" Luke Stirling? His grumpy new brother? *What the hell was he doing here?*

Luke glanced at him and grunted in response, then led the way back to the waiting room, where another surprise—actually, three more of them—

sat in the padded chairs. DJ, Sam and Mark, all masked, all of whom waved when they saw Danny.

He stared at them. "I… What are you all doing here?"

Lizzie's brow wrinkled. "Do you know them?"

Before he could answer, Sam stood up and crossed her arms as she stared Danny down. "We decided to get tested, too."

"But how…" How had they known he'd be here? He glanced at DJ, who lifted a brow. A swathe of emotion hit him. He'd told DJ about Emma, and the test he'd scheduled, sure, but never in a million years could he have imagined they'd show up here.

All of them. They were here to be tested, too. All of his wonderful siblings!

And Luke.

Danny's lungs contracted. Holy God. He wasn't sure how to react. He wasn't sure if he could. "You drove all the way here—?"

"We flew, actually," Luke said.

"Luke has a plane," DJ explained.

"Still…it's a long way."

Sam blew out a wet raspberry, one that made Emma's eyes go wide. "It's just a hop, skip and a jump. Anyway, we came for Emma. Once DJ told us about her, we had to meet her." Then Sam turned to Emma. "Hi. I'm Sam. I'm your aunt. Your father's sister. Though it's okay if you never heard about us because we just found out about you, too."

Emma gave her a curtsy. "Pleasure to meet you."

Which made them all laugh. And then his other siblings called out their names, as well, but they did it all at the same time, so Emma probably didn't hear them. She was, however, clearly delighted to be the center of attention.

Through all this, Danny's mind was awhirl. They came. All that way. To help him. No one had ever given him such a gift.

Not ever.

Why did his chest ache? Why did his throat tighten? Why did his eyes burn?

He turned to Lizzie and shook his head. "I didn't know they were coming," he whispered. "I can't believe they came."

"Of course, we came," Mark said, setting his hand on Danny's shoulder. "Emma's our family now, too."

"I think it's wonderful," Dr. Blake said. "If I had my way, everyone would be tested. Think how many kids we could help if everyone was on the registry."

He'd said that last part to Lizzie, and his words broke her out of her stunned silence. "Yes. Yes. Thank you," she said, shaking their hands, one by one. "Thank you. Thank you so much."

"It's our pleasure," Mark said with a grin.

DJ nodded. "We're family," he said.

Family.

It was absurd, but Danny couldn't stop grinning.

Nor could he stop the emotion from clogging his throat. For the first time in his life, he had a family to depend on.

Chapter Seven

Lizzie stared at Danny's family. His *family*.

Oh, not the woman who had raised him, but these warm, wonderful, generous souls who'd come all this way to help a little girl they'd never met. She shot a glance at Danny and her heart thudded at the joy and gratitude she saw in his eyes.

It was a truly magical moment. One she'd never imagined for Danny, certainly, but one she'd never imagined for Emma, either.

Her child hadn't just gained a daddy, she'd gained a clan.

A clan of good and decent people, who helped others and went out of their way—way out of their way—to support a family member. One they barely knew.

It was—

A tugging on her sleeve broke her from her bemused reverie.

"Mommy." And when she didn't respond quickly enough, Emma repeated, "Mommy. Mommy. Mommy."

"Yes, Emma, dear?" She touched Emma's forehead—her first instinctual thought. "Are you okay?"

"I'm hungry," she said in a plaintive voice.

"Oh, yes. I did promise you and Danny a snack after the test, didn't I?"

"Yes. You did. But I'm hungry for a sit-down meal."

"Do you want to go to the cafeteria?" The hospital had one and the food was pretty good…for hospital food.

"Oh, no." Emma rubbed her tummy. "I'm hungry for take-out food."

"Take-out food?" What on earth was she angling for?

"We should all go home and order take-out food." Lizzie followed her gaze to the attendant siblings, and it hit her like the gong of a church bell. Emma was a genius.

"Of course, darling," she said with a wink, and then she turned back to the others. "Hey, everyone. Emma, Danny and I are heading home to have a celebration lunch. Why don't you come with us? We'd love to get to know you all better."

"That sounds perfect," Sam said. "We even brought extra masks and a change of clothes, just in case."

"Really?"

At Lizzie's stunned response, Mark nodded. "We tried to read everything we could find on how to keep Emma safe. Let us know if we missed anything. Okay?"

Her heart warmed, swelled maybe. "Yes. Yes. Absolutely!"

And that was how Lizzie, Emma and Danny ended up across the dining room table—groaning with multiple Chinese take-out boxes—staring at Sam, Mark, DJ and Luke Stirling.

One would think this would be awkward.

One would be right.

Even Lizzie—who wasn't terribly sensitive about things like this—could tell there was a weird energy at the table.

She attempted to battle it by smiling at them as she said, "I can't tell you all how much your support means to us." She deliberately included Danny in this statement. "It is so generous of you."

"How could we not come?" Mark asked. Lizzie had already decided she liked him. He was so open and genuine. "If we can help Danny and Emma, of course, we will."

"But you just met Danny."

DJ frowned. "Stirlings stick together."

"You could have been tested closer to home." She

didn't mean to belabor the point, but she was still stunned that they'd come all the way here.

"Yes." Luke stared at her somberly. "But we wanted to meet Emma."

Emma, who had insisted on wearing her favorite tiara, preened.

"So," Sam gushed, an effort to break the tension, perhaps. "What's the dealio with that Dr. Blake?" she asked and waggled her eyebrows.

Lizzie blinked. "Well, he's Emma's doctor—"

Sam turned her attention to Emma and winked. "Quite the hottie, don't you think?"

Emma grinned. "He thinks my mom is pretty."

"Does he?" Sam's attention shifted to Danny.

Though he didn't respond, Lizzie felt him tighten at her side. "He, ah, went to the University of Washington," she said, apropos of nothing. And when she felt the heat of Danny's stare, she added, "He's very talented."

Emma nodded. "And he has a Jet Ski."

"Does he?" Mark asked, side-eying Danny, who was mauling a fortune cookie for some reason.

DJ widened his eyes with a fairly credible look of astonishment. "Lucky him."

"Sounds like fun," Sam said, deftly helping herself to another dumpling using chopsticks. "So, how old is he?" she asked.

Though the question was probably addressed to Lizzie, Emma answered as only Emma could. "Oh, he's very old. Almost as old as my mom." Then, when everyone laughed, she looked around the table in confusion. "Why is that funny?"

It was time to change the topic. "So," Lizzie said, "Danny was telling us about your ranch. It must be beautiful."

Apparently, this was a great choice as topics went. Mark's, Sam's and DJ's eyes brightened. Luke made a grunting noise, which Lizzie took as assent. He wasn't much of a talker like the others, she'd noticed.

"It's a hundred acres of the best cattle land in the Columbia Valley," Mark said, lifting his water glass. He turned his smile to Emma. "We have a big old house with a curving staircase." He leaned closer. "The banisters hardly ever have splinters. They're perfect for sliding down. Heck, we all did it when we were kids. You're gonna love it."

Emma turned wide-eyed to Danny. "Will I get to see it?" she asked. "Will I? Will I?"

"Of course," he said. And then, with a glance at Lizzie, he added, "When you're better."

Emma accepted this at face value and turned back to Mark. "So, do you have any bunnies?"

The expression on his face was priceless. He glanced at his siblings. "Um… We don't have bunnies."

"Except the ones running wild," Luke drawled.

"Ooh!" Emma shot him a smile that would melt granite. And, yes, even Luke's dour expression lightened. "Do you ever cuddle them?"

Lizzie tried very hard not to snort water through her nose. The thought of Luke cuddling anything was ludicrous.

He shifted in his seat. "I…ah. No. Can't say as I have."

Emma leaned closer and whispered, "They are so soft. You should try it sometime."

"Emma saw some bunnies at a petting zoo once. She fell in love," Lizzie explained.

"What's not to love?" the little girl exclaimed, and everyone laughed.

"We'll see if we can get some for you," Sam said. "I bet we could build a hutch."

"Better keep Mark's hounds away from them," Luke said.

Sam frowned at him. "Be nice."

Emma gasped melodramatically. Her eyes lit up. "You have *dogs*?"

"I have five right now," Mark told her.

"He rescues them and tries to get suckers to give them a home," Sam said. "They're all pretty mangy."

Mark made a serious face, but everyone could tell he was just playing. "Mangy dogs deserve love, too."

"I want a dog," Emma said, looking to her mother.

Fortunately, DJ noticed her consternation and changed the subject. "And what do you do, Lizzie?" he asked as he spooned a little more rice onto his plate.

"I'm an accountant," she said. "I'm on contract with a great company that lets me work from home so I can be with Emma."

"Really?" DJ asked with interest glinting in his eyes. "An accountant?"

"And what do you do, Danny?" Mark asked, ostensibly to keep the conversational balloon afloat.

Probably a misfire. Danny blinked and stared at Mark like a deer in the headlights. It bothered Lizzie to see him so anxious, even though she was curious as to how he would answer. What did he do now? Had he straightened his life out in more ways than one?

"What do I do?"

"Yeah." Luke put down his chopsticks. "You know. For a living?"

Danny dabbed his mouth with his napkin, then cleared his throat. "I guess I'm a rancher." He forced a grin. "At least for the next three years."

DJ lifted his glass and said, "I, for one, welcome you to the ranch. I'm sure we all do." He frowned at Luke. "Don't we?"

Luke grimaced—only the tiniest bit—but raised his glass, as well.

"I want to ranch," Emma said on a pout. "Can girls ranch, too?"

"Sam's one of the best wranglers we have," DJ said.

Mark grinned. "We call her the cow whisperer."

Emma turned to her brand-new aunt with wide eyes. "Do you ride horses and everything?"

Sam smiled at the little girl. "Sure do."

"I would like to ride a horse." This, of course, again, was directed at Lizzie.

Luke stepped in and saved her from answering. "Once we get you all better, you will." And then, after a quick glance in Lizzie's direction, "If your mom says it's safe."

Oh, he was good. She had to smile. "Emma, honey, if you're done eating, put your mask back on."

She rolled her eyes, but did so.

"What kind of things do you like to do, Ems?" Sam asked.

"I like to paint," Emma said. "I'm very good."

"I'll bet you are," Sam said.

Emma glowed at this praise. She leaned in and said proudly, "I can also spell words."

Mark raised his glass to her. "I have a multital-ented niece."

Everyone else concurred, which pleased Emma immensely. She slipped out of her chair and rounded the table, surveying her new relatives, one by one, as though she was a princess, deciding which one of her suitors to honor with her favor.

For some reason, she picked Luke. Quiet, gruff Luke.

To his shock, she climbed up onto his lap; he leaned away from her as he fumbled for his mask.

It was clear he wasn't used to having children climb on him, but to his credit, he handled the sudden intrusion well, rushing to cradle her weight and warily meeting her intense gaze. When she smiled at him, he made the same effort back.

And then she went and opened her mouth, as little girls often did. "How did you get hurt?" she asked, her gaze fixed on the scar ravaging one side of his face.

Oh, dear Lord. Lizzie nearly sank through the floor in mortification. "Emma, sweetie…" she began, but Luke waved her off.

His expression was somber, but sincere. He didn't look away. "I was a soldier, in another country. A bomb went off near me."

She looked at him. "Does it still hurt?"

A muscle in his cheek bunched. "Not there. Not anymore."

"Can I touch it?" Her finger hovered over his cheek.

Oh, God. "Emma! I'm so sorry," Lizzie said to Luke, but he shook his head. He had a hint of sadness in his tone when he replied to her.

"It's cool. Most people just look away or pretend I don't exist. I don't mind. Here." He took Emma's tiny hand in his and drew it to his face, sliding her finger along his scar. "What do you think?"

She shrugged. "It feels like my scars."

"And, hey," he said to Emma. "You can ask me anything, little one. Anytime you want."

"Anything?"

"Anything."

How funny was it that at this very moment, Lizzie should feel *connected* to this seemingly hard-hearted warrior? She hoped her smile conveyed her heartfelt appreciation.

It might have done, if Emma hadn't chimed in with a question. Any question but this one.

"I saw my mom and dad kissing last night. They tried to tell me kissing isn't gross when you're a grown-up. Do you think kissing is gross?"

Luke smiled then. A real smile, one that transformed his face, even with the mask on. "Oh, yeah," he said with a sly glance at Danny. "I think your mom and dad kissing is super gross."

Everyone at the table laughed, and Danny threw a fortune cookie at his brother, who caught it with one hand and held it aloft like he'd just won the world championship of sibling burns.

Amid the chuckles, Lizzie glanced at Danny then, and saw it there in his eyes. Just happiness. Happiness at being here, being part of this, with the people surrounding him. His joy was a palpable thing.

It was a new day for him, she realized. He wasn't alone in the world anymore.

And neither was she.

According to the nurse, it could take anywhere from a few days to a couple of weeks to get the results of the swab test they'd taken, and since they didn't know exactly when the conclusions would come in, they decided that Danny would drive back to the ranch with Mark in his truck, while the others flew back on Luke's plane.

These arrangements let Danny spend just a little more time with Emma and Lizzie before he had to leave. Before it was time for him to face his new life and go learn how to do something utterly alien to his nature: ranch. He'd never even seen a horse in Vegas that wasn't in a show, and his few experiences riding had been limited to that one gig accompanying paid day tours on themed trail rides outside the city. All the rest of it—roping and fence repairing and shoveling manure—was all pretty new, too. To say nothing of herding cattle.

But every time he looked at Emma, guilt snaked up his spine. Oh, he would stay in Seattle if he could. He would have slept on that uncomfortable sofa bed for a year if he had to, but he needed to pay off his debt and he really wanted to prove himself to DJ. And Emma needed that health care. Thankfully, Lizzie understood. Still, he promised to come back as soon as he could.

His farewell, when it was time for Danny and Mark to leave, was a reluctant one.

"Can I come and see you?" Emma asked as she clung to his neck.

"Sure, honey. As soon as the doctors say it's okay."

She pulled back and stared at him with her lower lip out and tears clinging to her lashes.

It nearly broke his heart.

But Lizzie laughed. "None of that, you little stinker," she said, ruffling Emma's curls.

Danny sent Lizzie a quizzical look.

"She's playing you," she explained.

"Am not!" Emma huffed a melodramatic sob.

"That lower lip is a dead giveaway. You always pretend-pout when you want your way."

Emma wrinkled up her face in outrage. "I'm not pretending. I really do want him to stay."

"I know, honey. But he has to go back to work. Standing there looking cute won't change his mind."

He pulled her into another hug. "I'll come back and see you as soon as I can. I promise. And I'll call you every night so we can tell each other about our day. How's that?"

"Okay." She closed her arms around his neck and clung to him, and the tears on his cheeks weren't pretend at all.

As hard as it was to leave, Danny really enjoyed the drive back with Mark. They had a great conversation—mostly Mark telling him stories about growing up on the ranch, Dorthea and Daniel Sr. and, of course, his own father.

It seemed surreal listening to stories about what a great dad Daniel Jr. had been. It didn't jibe at all with the stories his mother had told him. Granted, one had to consider the source. His mother had lied about many things. But one thing she hadn't lied about was how broke they'd been his whole life— a look in the fridge would attest to that—and how his loving father hadn't wanted anything to do with the boy he'd sired. Certainly not enough to help out financially when his mother was between shows.

Considering how Danny felt about Emma, after knowing her for such a short while, he just couldn't reconcile the two "dads" in his head. What kind of man could be so nurturing and loving to one son and cut the other off from everything? Even his love?

Granted, he'd learned to make a mean mac and cheese because of it.

In the end, he just decided not to dwell on it. The man was dead. There were no answers. No resolution. No reunion. No happy ending here.

Halfway home, Mark stopped at a roadside stand in Thorp, because he wanted to grab some cherries. And by cherries, he meant *cherries*. With the help of the staff, he started filling bags of them to take home. In the meantime, Danny wandered around the large barn-like store, checking out local honey, flavored nuts and popcorn made with blueberries. Then, he spotted the ice-cream counter. He had to get some, because it made him think of Emma. And because it made him think of Emma, he took a selfie of himself with his dripping double-scoop cone and sent it to Lizzie.

She sent back a laughing emoji and he grinned at the phone like a loon.

Funny how something so small could feel so good. Could make him feel…connected to her.

As he watched the employees of the store load Mark's cherries, he lapped at his cone and reflected on how good everything was. If things went the way he hoped, Emma would get her transplant. He had a job—with health-care benefits—and he and Lizzie were back together.

Well, not exactly back together. Not by a long shot. But they'd started communicating. That was a good thing. Maybe, if—when—Emma was healthy, they could try to work things out between them.

How awesome would it be if the two of them came to live in Butterscotch Ridge? When he could see them every day?

But a shiver walked through him as a familiar doubt surfaced. Nothing in his life had ever worked out. Why was he so sure this would? Should he even dare to hope?

Somewhere in the dark corners of his soul, he was afraid. Afraid that something bad was coming. And it was going to ruin everything. He didn't know if he could take it. Not if he lost Lizzie and Emma. Already, they meant everything to him.

He blew out a laugh. Wow. That had happened so fast, hadn't it? So fast and so hard. With little more than a smile and a kiss, they'd shattered his well-laid ramparts.

Mark slammed the tailgate and waved to Danny, who nodded and headed to the truck, chucking the remainder of his ice-cream cone in a nearby trash can along the way.

Well, he thought with a sigh. There was only one thing he could do, now that his heart was utterly exposed.

Make sure nothing bad happened.

Simple. Right?

Ranching was a lot harder than Danny imagined it would be. He'd thought it mostly involved riding around on a horse and checking fields and fences.

It wasn't that.

There was so much more to it than he'd ever realized. In addition to moving herds and repairing fences, there was feeding, calving, vet checks and lots of slopping around in the mud. He was surprised to discover how much he enjoyed it, even though he ended each day exhausted, dirty and aching everywhere. Some days were so busy, he completely forgot to worry about the money he owed Mikey, but he never forgot to worry about Emma. Just as he'd promised, he called her every day, no matter how busy he was.

It became part of his ritual. He'd lie back on the bed with the phone to his ear and listen to Emma talk about her day—with the occasional squeak when she was really excited about something. She'd tell him she hadn't been feeling well earlier, but felt better now. Then they'd tell each other really bad jokes and then laugh. At some point, she always went into a detailed accounting of everything she'd had to eat that day.

And then Lizzie would come on. His skin always prickled when he heard her calming voice. They'd share the events of their day. It was normal, boring couple chitchat. And he craved every minute of it.

Sometimes it would be bedtime when he called and then he got to help Lizzie read Emma a story. Of course, he'd had to order all her favorite story books so he could read along and do his parts.

Maybe that was just part of morphing into a dad. Allowing another, much smaller person to dictate your playlist. He didn't have much experience being a father, but he was pretty sure this wouldn't be the only thing Emma would change in his life.

All of a sudden, he thought of Christmas. Not the kind he'd had growing up, but the kind he'd seen on *The Brady Bunch* and other shows, where life was perfect. The kind he'd always wanted. The kind with flickering fires, heavily decorated and tinseled trees and presents. Lots of brightly wrapped presents for children to squeal over.

How wonderful would that be? And with Emma? And Lizzie?

His heart clenched. Oh, yes. That was what he wanted.

A healthy, happy, squealing child.

And a Christmas tree. He'd always wondered what that would be like.

His resolve—to convince Lizzie to come to the ranch when Emma was better—grew firm. More than that. Burned. Like an ache.

What if she didn't want to come? What if the doctors said they couldn't?

He'd made a commitment to DJ—well, to all of them, really—that he would stay here for three years. He owed them that. At least.

Because of them—all of them, even Luke—his life had changed for the better. His future looked promising. For once in his life.

Not that Luke wasn't a fly in the ointment—but something of a sibling rivalry had sprung up between them. It was funny, because the camaraderie with the others was so enjoyable. They were all impressed by his sincere efforts to learn and were eager to welcome him into the fold. Each day seemed to bring them closer.

Except Luke, of course. It was obvious he tried, but it was also clear he enjoyed the hell out of watching Danny struggle. He usually sat on his horse and grinned when Danny made a mistake, but the surly former marine really broke out of his shell whenever Danny unexpectedly parted ways with his steed. He'd stare down at Danny in the dust and howl with uncontained laughter.

In those instances, Luke was utterly unsympathetic.

Fortunately, after a couple of weeks, Danny was getting better on the horse. He hadn't fallen off in days. Well, if they didn't count the wobbly dismount this morning.

He groaned as he shouldered off his dirty shirt and headed for the bathroom. He'd really come to appreciate the merits of a really hot, long bath since he'd come here. He'd never really understood the allure before. He'd always been a shower guy. In, out, over.

Now he was a wallower.

He'd run the water as hot as he could stand and soak until his fingers pruned—or until the dinner bell rang—and he enjoyed every damn second.

Pulling off his boots, he was about to strip off his jeans—which were caked in mud—when his phone chirped. He glanced at the text message and his heart stuttered. Lifted.

It was from Dr. Blake.

It had to be the results of his test.

Excitement rippled through him, twined with a hint of anxiety.

But he didn't delay. He opened the message and read the results.

His breath caught as he stared at the screen.

He shook his head and read the message again, gutted. *No.*

The cell phone in his hand shook. He couldn't think. Couldn't breathe. And, after a moment, couldn't see.

Swiping his wrist over his eyes, he caught a damp breath. There had to have been a mistake. Someone made a mistake. He held his balled fist to his aching chest and dropped into the chair.

He wasn't a match. He was not an acceptable donor for his child. His baby.

With a damp sigh, he tromped to the window and stared out at a landscape that should calm his heart. It was peaceful out there, warm and brown. The leaves on the trees in the yard riffled in the breeze. The ripening hay swayed in the distance, harkening the onset of fall. Puffy clouds drifted peacefully, so white against that blue, blue sky.

And the air… He drew in a deep breath of sweet, clean oxygen.

How could one thing be so perfect and another be so horrible? How could he survive feeling so powerless about something that meant the world, that meant everything, to him?

His cell buzzed again and he glanced at it. His heart stopped.

Hell.

It was Lizzie.

What on earth was he going to say to her?

He couldn't talk to her now. He had to wait. Until he'd processed this.

With a groan at his own cowardice, he tossed the phone onto the bed and scrubbed at his face. How was he going to tell her?

The phone stopped buzzing and he collapsed in the chair. Oh, thank God—

The buzzing immediately resumed.

His gut clenched.

Dammit all. He had to take the call. He *had* to tell her. Now. He lurched for the phone and answered before he changed his mind.

"Lizzie." He was well aware his voice was choked.

"Did you hear? Danny? Did you hear? *They found a match for Emma!*" she cried.

A tsunami of emotion careened through his chest, stealing his breath. "What?" he said. A stupid response to this news, but it was all he could muster.

"They found a donor, Danny. Can you believe it? Oh, they still have to do a couple more tests, but Dr. Blake says it looks really good. Isn't that great news?"

It was. It was…a miracle.

"So great." Gratitude rushed through him. Never mind that he'd wanted to be the one—indeed, had been sure he would be the one. All that really mattered was that Emma had a bone-marrow donor. She had a chance now.

"I'm so excited. I wish you were here." The connection was a little tinny. She sounded so far away. He wished he was there, too. "Would you like to speak to Emma?"

"Yes. Yes, please."

"Daddy?" His heart soared at the sound of her little-girl voice, but stayed elevated because of that word. He loved it. *Daddy.*

"Hi, sweetie."

"Did you hear?"

"I sure did, honey. That's so great. What are you doing to celebrate?"

"Wearing my tiara."

He chuckled. "Of course you are."

"And Aunt Nan made a cake. I wish you were here."

"I wish I was there, too, honey. I'll come over soon."

"Promise?"

He hated to make a promise when he wasn't sure he could keep it, but this time he knew, come hell or high water, he'd keep this one. "I promise."

"Yay," she cheered. "Oh. Mommy wants the phone back. Here."

"Danny?"

The sound of her voice soothed and excited him. It always did. He leaned all the way back in the chair. "Yeah, Lizzie?"

"I'm sorry. My phone is almost out of juice. I just wanted to…oh, I don't know. Talk to you again. I'm so happy, Danny."

"Me, too."

"The tough part starts now, though."

"Now?" Yikes. Hadn't this been hard enough already?

"Yes. We'll be prepping Emma for the transplant."

"I'll come over." He was ready to go, like, now.

She chuckled. "I only told you that to prepare you for what's coming, that's all. Not that you're not welcome to come. You are. Whenever—" She broke off awkwardly. "I'd love to see you…"

"Well, I want to be there for as much of it as I can. I would like to come. As soon as I can. I just need to clear it with DJ."

"Of course."

Wait. Was that a sob hidden in the words? God, he hated phone conversations. He'd much rather be face-to-face. Static hummed, but he couldn't think of anything to say.

As always, she came through. "Um, how are you enjoying ranching?"

He huffed a laugh. Surely not one of relief. "My butt hurts."

"Does it?" He could hear the amusement in her voice.

"Apparently, I'm not very good at staying on horses."

She did laugh then, probably imagining his slick Las Vegas persona trying to stay astride a bucking bronc.

"I'm learning, though. And loving this place." He cleared his throat. "It's a beautiful place. To live. Maybe even to, ah, raise a child."

"Is it?" Ah. Yes. He heard the smile in her words.

"It is. But there's more."

She paused. "Okay."

"I'm officially on the payroll. That means I have medical coverage. DJ suggested that, well, that I add Emma as a dependent. They accept preexisting conditions." And, when she didn't respond, he added, "I mean, she *is* my daughter."

"Danny." Lizzie exhaled on a gust. She sounded out of breath. "Yes. Yes. Oh, yes. Please do put Emma on your insurance. That would be…that would be… Yes. Thank you." This last bit was a whisper, but he heard her.

Chapter Eight

Lizzie ended the call, then closed her eyes and steadied her head as it spun.

Those two words made a world of difference. *Health insurance.* The coverage she had for herself and Emma, which she had to buy herself because she was a contract employee, was adequate for most issues. But the cost of a bone-marrow transplant was more than her plan would cover. Secondary coverage would be amazing.

It would be so wonderful not to have to worry about more debt. A huge burden, finally relieved.

Funny, wasn't it? Danny Diem had once been an immature guy who avoided commitment and lived for the moment, without any thought for the future. But he had changed.

Now, he was thoughtful and kind, working hard to fit in with his new family. He was certainly ready and willing to step up and try to be a father to Emma in every way.

She thought back to that kiss, the night he stayed over before getting tested. How his lips had felt against hers. Was it wrong to assume he was interested in rekindling their relationship, as well? She tried to ignore the ribbon of delight that wove through her at the thought. It was too early for such ideas, no matter how tempted she was to lean into them. No matter what Lizzie wanted, Emma had to come first.

Watching Nan cut a slice of cake and hand the plate to Emma, she smiled. It was a charming sight—Emma elated, playful, childlike once more. How wonderful would it be if, after all this, she could have a normal childhood again? But what would that look like?

Danny had mentioned how lovely it was in Butterscotch Ridge, what a great place it was to raise children. Had he been hinting that they move there when Emma got better?

He hadn't been specific. Was it silly for her to start imagining a life with him? Other than one brief kiss, he hadn't given her a clue. It was far too soon for that. Wasn't it?

She wasn't sure, but her heart wanted that. Wanted that more than it should.

"Mommy?" Emma thrust a slice of cake under her nose.

"Thank you, honey."

"There's no ice cream." An apology, perhaps. Or maybe an indictment of Lizzie's shopping skills.

"Cake is fine. Mmm. Is this chocolate?"

"With chocolate icing." She hadn't needed to mention that. It was all over her face.

"Are you even using a fork?" Lizzie chuckled as she used her napkin to wipe the smears from Emma's cheeks. And her fingers. And that spot behind her knee.

"I licked the bowl," she said proudly. "What should we do next? To celebrate?"

Nan grinned. "I vote for a bath."

Lizzie chuckled at Emma's disgruntlement. "I second." Because really. Frosting was everywhere.

Later, as Lizzie tucked Emma into bed and kissed her good-night, she felt that flare of hope again. She couldn't wait until Danny joined them in Seattle, and this time, he'd be with her every step of the way.

As Danny headed down the stairs for supper, he was in a great mood, and bursting with the news. It was a testament to his growing relationship with his siblings that he knew they'd be just as happy as he was to hear that Emma had found a donor.

When Mark saw him, he flashed a brilliant grin. Actually, Sam, DJ and Luke—*Luke*—were grinning, as well. Since Danny hadn't just fallen off a horse, *that* was not normal.

"What's up?" he asked as he took what had become his usual seat. Right next to his gruff brother, as it happened.

"We have news," Sam said.

Luke snorted. "*We* have news?"

"Oh?" Another glance around the table at those smiles, and something prickled on Danny's nape.

Sam nodded. "We got a call today—"

"Just tell him already," DJ said.

"Okay fine," Sam muttered to her older brother. "The doctor called to say they found a donor for Emma!" She looked so proud of herself, he hated to burst her bubble.

"Yeah," he said. "I already know."

Odd, then, that none of their smiles dimmed. Luke's, in fact, widened. "But do you know who the donor is?" he asked.

Danny stilled, stared at him.

"Just tell him already," Dorthea snapped from the end of the table. "It's Luke."

Sam nodded. "It is. It's Luke. Isn't that wonderful?"

And what could he say? Because it *was* wonderful. Even if it was Luke. "It is. It is wonderful. Thank you all, again, for getting tested." He leaned over and hesitated, then gave his brother his hand because Luke seemed to be more of a handshake kind of guy. To his surprise, Luke grabbed him in an awkward one-armed embrace, then shoved him away, saying, "We told you. Stirlings take care of each other."

"This is going to change things," DJ said as Danny was still processing a hug from Luke. *From Luke.* "They want Luke to come in for more tests." He waved his hand. "I think you should go, too. Lizzie and Emma will need you."

"My three months isn't up yet." It was only fair to remind him.

DJ shook his head. "You don't need to worry about that."

"I can't help worrying about a debt that needs paying." People who didn't worry about debts to Mikey tended to end up in traction.

"Well, I, ah, already took care of that matter."

"What?" Danny gaped at him. His pulse thudded in his temple. "When?"

"The first night you arrived." DJ grinned.

Another tsunami of incredible relief and gratitude rolled over him.

His brother grinned. "I also paid off the repairs on your car. George is delivering it next week. Had to send out for parts."

"Oh, man. My 'Vette. Thank you." It might seem odd for a man to get worked up over an old car, but Danny had always loved that 'Vette. Even though it was kind of a clunker, it was the first thing he'd bought with money he'd earned. He'd kissed Lizzie for the first time in that car. It mattered to him.

How incredibly wonderful that DJ had taken care of that, as well as the monumental debt that had been weighing on him.

Oh, he couldn't stop himself. He hugged DJ again. It was a hug that went on for a while. There might have been some manly sniffles, too.

"I...ah... Thank you. Thank you very much."

DJ disentangled himself, caught Danny's gaze and held it for a moment. "You don't need to thank me. We're family. We're all in this together."

The next day, Luke flew them both to Seattle in his plane, which was a little terrifying, because Danny had never been in a plane that small. He was white-knuckled most of the flight, which Luke found amusing. Fortunately, his brother remained silent for most of the trip, leaving Danny to his thoughts.

He was still gobsmacked by DJ's munificence. He'd done everything he'd promised, despite the fact that Danny hadn't yet met his obligation. In the past, his inclination would have been to distrust such a man and his motives, and to fortify himself from impending betrayal. How strange it was that those suspicions seemed ludicrous with these people. DJ had always been straight with him. As had Mark, Sam and, to be honest, Luke, as well.

It was strange and wonderful to trust people, and

to have their trust, as well. It made him want to be a better man. Lizzie and Emma made him want to be a better man, too. It was a scary thought, but the thought of disappointing them was scarier.

Lizzie met them at the airfield. He wanted to kiss her, but held back. He regretted it immediately, though. When would a celebratory kiss have been more appropriate?

They drove straight to the hospital as Luke had tests scheduled, as well as a briefing on what to expect, and Lizzie had made an appointment with Dr. Blake so he could brief Lizzie and Danny on the process to come. They dropped Luke at the lab and headed upstairs.

As the elevator ascended, Danny took Lizzie's hand. She didn't object, which he took as a good omen. "You okay?"

She shot him a wobbly smile. "Nervous."

He huffed a laugh. "Me, too." Nervous and excited. And relieved he didn't have to do this alone. He had Lizzie by his side.

They sat in the pair of chairs in front of the doctor's desk and held hands as he explained what was coming next. The only reason Danny was able to follow along was because he'd spent much time surfing the internet for articles on aplastic anemia, bone-marrow transplants and the like.

"What we're going to do is an allogeneic stem-cell transplantation," the doctor said. "It's highly successful, with a seventy-five-percent survival rate. Our goal is to induce remission, to eliminate bleeding complications and neutropenic infections."

Danny nodded, as though he understood all the words. Didn't matter. He'd researched this enough to get the gist.

"We'd like to schedule the transplant as soon as possible," the doctor added. "There's some prep work for Emma to get through first, which takes about ten days."

"What does it involve?" Danny asked.

"We're going to give Emma some treatments to prepare her for the transfusion, including a reduced intensity conditioning—"

Danny frowned. Oh, wait. He was going too fast. "Reduced intensity conditioning?"

The doctor nodded. "We need to prepare her body for the transplant so she won't reject Luke's bone marrow, and make room for the new bone marrow to grow. But since she's already compromised, we use smaller doses. If necessary, we'll do a TBI—total body irradiation. And then after the transplant, of course, she'll be on medicine to help her use the new marrow."

Lizzie nodded. "And the side effects?"

Dr. Blake sighed. "The usual. Nausea and vomiting. Diarrhea. Fatigue. Sore mouth. Skin sensitivity."

"Will she lose her hair?" Lizzie whispered, as though, if she spoke louder, Emma might hear. Danny's heart gave a painful thud.

"She could." Lizzie's hold on Danny's hand tightened. "But Emma's strong. She can handle anything if she's mentally prepared."

"Right." The message was clear. Prepare Emma for losing her hair.

"Then, after the transplant, we'd like to keep her in hospital for at least a month and then do regular tests for six or so, depending on how she's doing."

"Okay." A nod. Danny glanced at Lizzie. There was tension painted on her face. He hoped his rising anxiety didn't show. Had it been like this for her, for so long? All alone?

He could barely stand the churning in his gut as he contemplated his baby girl suffering one treatment after another. How on earth had Lizzie managed it all by herself?

The thought broke his heart, but strengthened his resolve. From now on, he'd be here for her. And for Emma. For everything.

No matter what it took.

That night, there was a party. Granted it consisted of only five people—everyone wore masks—and a stuffed rabbit, but there was pizza and root beer and ice cream. Emma was over the moon to have her uncle Luke on hand. It was clear she adored him, which warmed Lizzie's heart.

Not as much as it moved her to see Emma and Danny together, though.

"Are you all right?" Nan asked while they were clearing the table.

Lizzie glanced over at where Luke, Danny and Emma were playing old maid. "I'm just happy, I guess."

Nan nodded. "It's been a long time coming. And you deserve some happiness."

"Thanks, Nan." She pulled her sister into her arms and hugged her. "You've been great through all this, you know."

Her sister grinned. "Yeah. I know. I'm awesome."

"You are." Lizzie turned back to the card game, which, in her opinion, was starting to get a little too unruly. "Emma Jean," she said. "Time for bed."

They had agreed that Emma would sleep with Lizzie and let Luke have her room, but now that it was actually bedtime, she changed her mind.

"I want to have a sleepover with Aunt Nan," she said. A sleepover in Aunt Nan's room was a special treat, but since Nan was willing, and they all agreed Emma deserved a treat, Lizzie agreed.

After everyone else turned in, Lizzie and Danny sat up talking. It was so…nice. Just the two of them, there on the sofa. Talking. About nothing. And everything.

She reached out and took his hand, marveling in its strength and warmth. "Have I told you lately how glad I am you're here?" It needed to be said.

He smiled. "I'm glad I'm here, too. I can't tell

you how much it means to have you in my life again. And Emma. She's just…" He shook his head.

"Yeah." Lizzie took a sip of her wine. "She is."

"I'm still absorbing what it means to be a father. This is all new to me. But one thing's clear."

"Hmm?"

"You, Lizzie… You're a great mom."

Such simple words. But they hit home. She turned away as a wave of emotion swept over her. "I can't tell you how—" she swallowed her sob "—how hard it's been."

He stilled, took her hand. "How…"

"Yes?" she prompted when he didn't continue.

"How are you so…brave?"

She swallowed heavily. Tears stung at her eyes. Brave? Hardly. She lifted a shoulder in a shrug. "When your child depends on your being there— being strong—it's your job to be there for her. So you either do what you need to do, or you don't."

"Hey." He touched her chin and guided her back to his earnest gaze. "Don't cry. I'm here. I'm here now."

His lips were gentle on her cheek. Nuzzling away her tears. But they found their way to her lips and he kissed her. Slowly. Softly. Perfectly. "I'm here now," he murmured. "Right here with you."

She touched her lips to his, letting him know she wanted more. As he gave in to her, she opened her mouth to him. Drank him in. His fingers stroked her hair, her cheek, so gently, as he kissed her. She needed more, so she pressed against him.

When he cupped her breast, an amazing jolt of electricity hit her. It sizzled down her spine and she moaned. He circled her nipple and it swelled. Delight sluiced through her. She buried her fingers in his shirt. God, it had been so long. Too long. Her body *tingled*.

His hot mouth made his way down her shoulder, right to that spot that made her collapse like a gooey soufflé.

"Maybe we should…" She waved toward her bedroom. It wouldn't do to *collapse* all over the living room floor.

"Oh. Yeah." He stood and held out a hand, tugging her to her feet. And they kissed all the way to her room.

Danny's mind spun. Ah, Lizzie. She was warm and willing in his arms. It had been so long, he had wanted her for so long, he could barely contain himself.

It didn't help that she seemed to be just as needy as he was. Her lips were warm, her kisses drugging. His sanity waned.

She released his mouth to nibble on a spot beneath his ear that she knew made him wild. "Hush, now," she said when he growled in response. "We don't want to wake anyone up."

He noted his agreement by pulling her closer and

closing his mouth over hers. She stilled. Stroked his shoulders. Ran her fingers up into his hair. Then her nails.

Shivers walked over his skin as pleasure flooded him. "Damn, Lizzie," he whispered into her neck. She was so sweet there, right at that spot. He couldn't resist a taste. A suckle. She moaned. Yeah. She'd always been tender there.

He explored more as she writhed against him, eyes closed, chin tipped high so he could reach the spot she wanted, craved.

"I've missed this," she whispered.

"Me, too." He dipped his head and caught her nipple through her blouse in another wet suckle.

"Oh, Danny." She arched against him. It felt very much like bliss.

"Lizzie." He pulled off her shirt and her bra and found her again. This time skin to skin. As he tasted her, licked and sucked and nipped, he stroked down her hip, her thigh, the backside of her knee and back up again, slowly finding his way up under her skirt to the warm, wet heart of her. She stilled when he touched her there, gently, on that hard nub. He could have sworn it throbbed beneath his touch. But he had no time to contemplate that, because she opened to him.

His heart pounded. Everywhere. Ah, but it felt good.

He slid his fingers inside and his breath stalled. She was ready. So ready.

It nearly killed him, but he had to break away and meet her gaze.

Hers was annoyed. "Why'd you stop?"

"I just... Are we ready to do this?"

"What?"

Uh-oh. Now she was really annoyed. "I mean, we've been taking it slow. Are you...? Are you ready to do this?"

She stared at him, and her expression softened. She ran her fingers through his hair. "Yes, Danny. I'm ready."

He grinned at her. "It's been way too long, Lizzie."

She rubbed her nose against his. "It has been."

"I'd really like to take this slow—"

"Oh, please don't."

"But it's been a really long time."

"Hey." She grabbed him by the chin. "Shut up and kiss me."

So he did.

He kissed her everywhere.

He kissed her until she was begging and pleading, until she totally forgot to be quiet.

And then, when he entered her, glorying in the amazing feel of her body around his, they both lost complete and utter control.

It was wild. It was hard and it was fast.

It was magnificent.

Transcendent, in fact.

They barely even heard Luke banging on the wall.

* * *

When Lizzie woke up the next morning, she was alone in her bed. She had no idea why her mood drooped. Of course he'd left her in the night. What had she expected?

Certainly not to find him in the kitchen with Emma making bacon. He shot her a broad grin. "Good morning," he said.

"Mommy! We made breakfast."

"I see that." She wandered to the counter and helped herself to a crispy slice. "Mmm," she said as she crunched it. Just the way she liked it.

Danny brought her a steaming mug of coffee, which he presented with a kiss. Lizzie was surprised, but his affection was not unwelcome. "Thank you."

"Did you sleep well?" he asked in a smooth tone.

"Yeah," Luke said gruffly from behind her. "Did you sleep well? Because I didn't."

She whipped around and shot him a horrified glance. The fact that he was grinning didn't cool the heat on her cheeks.

"Why didn't you sleep, Uncle Luke?" Emma asked.

Lizzie frowned at Luke. His grin widened. "Oh, Emma Jean. I think there were bunnies nearby. They made a lot of noise."

Emma gasped. "You think there were bunnies?"

"Yes," Luke said with a knowing glance at his brother. "I do."

"Hey," Lizzie said on a gust of breath. "Who wants pancakes?" And, thank heaven, that was the end of that conversation.

They'd barely finished breakfast when Dr. Blake called to share that Luke's final tests were all good and he'd been cleared for the procedure. Because the doctors wanted to move forward as quickly as possible, they asked that Emma come to the hospital to begin the challenging preparation for the transplant right away.

This was great news, but it was still difficult for Danny, watching his daughter pack her little suitcase with books and videos. And her favorite tiara, even though it had to be sanitized.

It was even more difficult leaving her at the hospital. Especially when she clung to his neck and smooched his cheek and said, "I love you, Daddy."

Something caught in his throat, swelled in his chest as he heard those beautiful words. The most beautiful words in the world.

"I love you, too, honey. I love you so much."

He held her then, until the nurse came in and gently reminded him of the visitation rules on the floor. Lizzie got to stay, because she was taking the first night with Emma. He hugged her, too, before he left the room. "You going to be okay?" he asked in an undertone.

She smiled. "I'll be fine. I've done this before. Don't worry."

"See you tomorrow?"

"Of course." And then, to his delight, she kissed him. It wasn't a long, lingering thing, but it was enough to let him know that she wouldn't object to such displays of affection in front of others, which was a damn good sign.

When Emma went into the hospital, they all took turns staying the night with her—Danny, Lizzie, Nan and Luke—who planned to stay with them until Emma's procedure.

Danny quickly learned not to expect any sleep on his nights because Emma's room was like Grand Central Station. Nurses and doctors came in and out all night, taking her temperature or adjusting an IV, and the machines beeped constantly.

But, he reminded himself, he was here for her. To make sure she felt safe. And he prayed that in those times when she woke up and saw him there, not sleeping in the uncomfortable chair-bed by the window, she knew he was there to protect her.

There were good times and bad as Emma went through the preparation, and as difficult as it was for Danny to help his child through bouts of nausea, to coax her to eat when she lost her appetite or hold her when she cried, he was, at least, happy to have the chance do it. For Emma, and to spare Lizzie, as well. And humbled to have this chance to be with his child. He vowed he'd do everything he could to make sure she got through this. Knowing as he did that there was only so much he *could do*.

Luke's *aspiration*—as the doctors called it—was on a Thursday. Since Lizzie had stayed the night before with Emma, Nan drove them to the hospital. Danny could tell that Luke was a little nervous, but when he brought it up, his brother snorted, "Bah. This is nothing." He glanced at Danny and added, "Sometime, when we've had a couple belts, ask me about my adventures at Walter Reed." Danny knew Luke had been severely wounded in battle and spent months in the military hospital, but he didn't know the details. This, however, felt like an invitation to a conversation, which was all to the good.

"I'll do that," he said.

Luke nodded. "Just make sure there's alcohol."

Once they arrived at the hospital, and got sanitized and masked, gloved and gowned, they headed for Emma's room in the isolation unit. Lizzie stood and set aside the magazine she was reading when she saw him. It took two steps for her to come into his arms, but she did. "You okay?" he whispered into her hair.

"Yeah. It's just…"

"I know." He pulled back and smiled into her eyes. "She'll be fine. It'll be okay soon."

"Notice he doesn't say *I'll* be fine," Luke muttered, pointing a thumb at them.

Emma laughed. Then she sobered and stared at Luke with wide eyes. "You will be fine," she said in the manner of Obi-Wan Kenobi persuading an Imperial stormtrooper.

"Thanks, little one," he said, patting her through the plastic. Clearly, he didn't expect her to take his hand, but he allowed it. Danny even thought he saw a return squeeze.

When the nurse came to collect Luke to prepare for his procedure, Emma clung to his hand.

"Hey, hey, little one. Don't be scared," he said.

"I'm not scared." She shook her hair and her thinning curls bounced. "I just don't want *you* to be scared."

His eyes widened. "Should I be scared?" he asked, not so jokingly.

"Don't worry," she said. "I've done this before."

Luke blinked. "Have you? Did it hurt?"

She shot him a brilliant grin. "Not while you're sleeping."

Danny went with Luke to be there for him during his procedure, while Lizzie stayed with Emma. It was the least he could do, he figured.

He was past feeling hurt over not being able to be the one to donate to his own daughter. Now that he knew his brother a little better, he'd come to understand that Luke's crusty outer shell was just his armor. Underneath was a flesh-and-blood man, wounded and wanting connection, just like anyone else. In fact, under that crusty outer shell was a damned fine man.

Funny how Emma had seen that from the start. It was an incredibly insightful observation for a child. Or maybe kids just saw things more clearly than world-weary adults.

Regardless, she certainly did have a special place in her heart for Luke. But then, so did Danny nowadays.

Not that Luke needed to know that.

At least, not yet.

Luke came through with flying colors, just as Emma predicted. Not only was he fine, but he also even insisted on visiting Emma before they left that evening so she could see for herself. Everyone, however, noticed his disgruntlement when the hospital was adamant that he be ferried to the hospital door in a wheelchair. His accentuated limp, however, he utterly ignored. "It's nothing," he said when anyone brought it up. "Nothing."

Even though it was *nothing*, the doctors said he shouldn't do strenuous labor—like lifting bales of hay and wrassling two-thousand-pound steers—so there was no need for him to return to the ranch. Besides, he wanted to stay for the transplant.

Lizzie was happy to have him. In fact, it was a luxury to have Danny and Luke with her. They were a great distraction from her worries. Just watching the two of them awkwardly bond was worth the price of admission. It warmed her heart, sure, but it also made her laugh. The two of them were so alike, even if *they* couldn't see it.

* * *

The night before Emma's procedure was rough. The nurses recommended she get a good night's sleep, because the next few days could be challenging, but Emma was too apprehensive to settle. Funny little thing. She'd been stalwart all along, even when her hair started falling out in clumps—as long as she could still wear a tiara, she'd said, she'd be fine. But now that the day of reckoning had arrived, she was worried. And today's infusion wouldn't even hurt.

Lizzie couldn't blame her. She was worried about what would happen next, too. Thankfully, Danny insisted on staying that night, even though the only place for him to sleep was the mat on the window seat—but he didn't sleep much, either. Every time Lizzie awoke, it was to find him gazing at Emma, or pacing the floor. She knew he was fretting, as well.

The procedure was an infusion of Luke's bone marrow into her bloodstream via the central line they'd put in for this purpose, but that was the easy part. Emma could have a negative reaction to the infusion, or even reject the transplant itself. Either could be fatal. They all knew Emma wouldn't be out of the woods until they knew the transplant had grafted and she was making her own, healthy marrow.

Too soon that morning, the nurses came to prep Emma for her infusion. Her parents weren't allow to hug her, so they had to be satisfied with *air-fives*, as Emma called them. They threw kisses and told her how much they loved her. And then they sat next to her bed as she was lightly sedated and the infusion began. And they waited. This was the hardest part. It always was, the waiting.

Emma's nurse kept checking on her infusion and Dr. Blake came in several times, reassuring them that everything was going smoothly. But this time, things were decidedly different for Lizzie. This time she wasn't alone as she waited. She had Danny beside her, holding her hand, and Nan and Luke had come for moral support, though they waited in the family room and texted periodically to send notes and jokes, to help keep their spirits up. The company didn't miraculously banish her anxiety, but having them there helped tremendously.

It seemed as though hours had gone by when Danny's fingers tightened slightly around hers. Lizzie's eyes flew open. They stood as Dr. Blake came into the room to check on Emma's progress.

"Well?" Danny said, his voice a warble.

Dr. Blake set his hand on Danny's shoulder. "I spoke to Rachel. She said everything went well. Now we watch her carefully, just as we talked about. She should be awake soon, and I'm sure she'll be happy to see her mom and dad here."

After Dr. Blake left, promising to check back in a few hours, they gave Luke the okay to call the family and give them an update. All of the Stirlings had been pretty adamant about being kept in the loop.

Lizzie's heart caught as she looked at her little girl. She seemed so small on the bed. There were smudges under her eyes. Her lashes made dark arcs on her cheeks.

"Baby." Lizzie stroked the damp tufts of hair off her forehead. Emma's eyes fluttered open. "How you feeling?"

Her smile was wobbly. "Where's Uncle Luke?"

Behind Lizzie, Danny smiled. "He's on the phone, telling everyone how great you did."

"I did great?"

Danny stepped closer. "Of course you did. We're all so proud of you."

That was about all they had time to say, because Emma was clearly tired, and began to doze. Far too soon.

The nurse urged them to get something to eat so that they could be back when Emma awoke and she promised to text them if there were any changes. They headed to the hospital cafeteria for a late lunch with Luke and Nan. Lizzie was glad for the company. She was staying with Emma tonight, and wasn't ready to be alone with her thoughts. Not just yet. Danny had wanted to stay, too, but the doctors insisted on one parent only from now on, to decrease the chance of an infection and even then, Emma would be in isolation for at least two weeks and under close supervision for the next thirty days.

When the others left that night, Lizzie walked them to the front door of the hospital. Danny dropped his arm around her shoulder. He kissed her. Gently. Sweetly.

"It's over," he said on a sigh.

And she smiled.

Because the fun had just begun, and he didn't even know it yet.

Luke was reluctant to leave when the time came, but he was needed at the ranch. Especially with Danny staying to help out during Emma's recuperation. He seemed as broken up about leaving as Lizzie was watching him go—even Danny got a little emotional, though he hid it well. Luke promised to come back soon for a visit.

There were a few scary days after the transplant when it looked like the procedure didn't take. Everything from temperature spikes and blood tests showed Emma was slow to respond. She had difficulty keeping food and water down, which required multiple IVs and the occasional feeding tube. She slept nearly all the time.

Lizzie didn't sleep much at all. It wasn't just the worrying. Every parent of a hospitalized child knew the drill. Even though Emma was in a sterile room, there were doctors and nurses, mostly nurses, in and out of the room all night. And if Emma's oxygen levels dropped below ninety, an alarm would sound. And when her saline drip needed changing, an alarm would sound. And, for a million other reasons, an alarm would sound. By the end of the first week, she was dizzy with fatigue.

Danny and Lizzie had an argument over stale doughnuts and coffee in the cafeteria when she refused to let him take over. He was worried about *her* health, too, he insisted. It wasn't until she caught her own reflection in the mirror—and it was spooky—that she relented and let him stay with Emma every other night.

And, of course, she was glad she had. Not just because she had a chance to catch up on her sleep, but because Danny wanted, and *needed*, to be a part of this. Other than Nan, Lizzie hadn't had anyone else to rely on. She'd gotten used to that so naturally it was hard to make this adjustment. But it was important for her to allow him in. Emma needed her dad, too.

Wasn't that partly what she'd hoped for when she'd sought him out?

Lizzie's stress began to wash away when Emma turned a corner. Both her red and white blood-cell counts started to rise. She was finally able to keep down solid food. She began to show an interest in cartoons.

In fact, after they'd passed that sketchy period, the doctors seemed very pleased with Emma's response to Luke's bone marrow. Though they were being conservative with their prognosis, they said, they felt confident moving Emma out of isolation.

There was even talk that she might be home in time for Christmas.

As her blood counts continued to rise, her energy increased, too, and soon, she refused to be confined to the bed, as the doctors had ordered. More than once, Lizzie came into her room to see her perched on the wide windowsill watching cars zoom by on the road below, or she'd had to search the ward to find her daughter. She was usually found cajoling the nurses for ice cream.

Fortunately, she had Danny to help her look when she needed him. She had Danny to help her with everything. On the occasional night when Nan stayed with Emma, they held each other close all night long.

As difficult a time as it was, she was utterly grateful to have him by her side.

Although she couldn't help wondering…what would happen when Emma was all better? What would he expect or need or want from her then? Would he still be by her side?

Chapter Nine

Luke flew over to visit a lot during the month Emma was in hospital, once a week, at least. Sometimes Mark, DJ or Sam would come with him. A couple of times, they all flew out together.

Once, because she'd heard Emma's hair was falling out, Sam brought a bunny hat she'd hand-knitted. It had two fluffy ears and a black nose in the front. Emma loved it. It wasn't long before she refused to walk—only hopped—when she wore it.

It was a tremendous boon to Lizzie to have this extra moral support. But there was more to it than that. She'd figured out long ago that hospital life could often become tedious—eating in the cafeteria for days on end, washing your hair in the sink, sleeping on the chairs that promised to convert into comfy beds…and *lied*. Having visitors helped Lizzie keep her sanity.

And then, of course, there were the times when all the Stirlings were over—and nothing was sane. On those nights, Danny, Luke, Sam—and whoever else had come—would pile in her car after visiting Emma and head back to the condo to hang out for hours. How had she not known family get-togethers were such fun?

Growing up, it had just been Nan and Lizzie. Their parents had been college professors. A wild night for them had been *maybe* a glass of wine. Was it any surprise their daughters turned out the same?

Well, when the Stirlings stayed over, nothing was tame. Meals were boisterous, and conversation and laughter flowed well into the night. Sometimes it was about Emma—and here was a group of people who were avidly interested in her baby pictures— but sometimes it was about the ranch, or the town of Butterscotch Ridge.

They never seemed to run out of things to say to each other. Even Danny was slowly getting drawn into their circle.

Lizzie even found herself slowly bonding with Danny's forthright sister, Samantha, who proved to be both kind and funny underneath her sharp-edged snark.

"Do you guys do game night every evening?" Lizzie asked one night after a particularly cross-eyed game of charades. Because everyone was over, Nan had insisted Lizzie and Danny both have the night off and she'd taken a shift.

Sam chuckled. "We're usually too pooped most nights. But we can do game nights when you come to the ranch if you want." The comment was a casual one, but it made Lizzie's throat close. She hadn't been invited to come to the ranch. Not precisely. Naturally, she glanced at Danny. She couldn't help it.

Silence simmered.

Mark looked at Danny, then at her, and asked, "You *are* coming to the ranch. Aren't you?"

DJ nodded. "We assumed you were coming. Once Emma's better."

They all stared at her with that distinct *Stirling* look. Like birds of prey waiting for the twitch of a titmouse.

"Oh. Yes." Lizzie swallowed the lump in her throat. "I assumed we would visit…"

"Visit?" Sam's jaw dropped. "What? I thought you and Emma were *moving* to BR." For some reason, she glared at Danny.

"He hasn't asked her," Luke snorted.

Danny winced. "I haven't brought it up yet. We've been *busy*. Have you noticed?"

Her heart thudded. Her mouth went dry. "Ask me what?"

Something hummed between them, some energy, some snapping tension. After a moment, he tipped his head sideways and gave her a hesitant smile, one that made her chest warm. "Would you... and Emma like to come and live on the ranch?" She stared at him until he gulped at her lack of response. He gestured to his siblings. "With us?" he added in a squeak.

With us? He meant the whole family.

Her mind spun a little. Probably because she'd been expecting a different question and dreading it. And wanting it and not wanting it. But he hadn't asked that. Of course, he hadn't asked *that*. This was Danny Diem. The man to whom marriage had always been a forbidden subject. Still, it took a second for her to process the shift.

Would they like to come and live at the ranch?

No doubt the fresh air and absence of crowds would be good for Emma as she continued to heal. Being near her father would be good, too. Emma was crazy about Danny.

And so was she, Lizzie had to admit. Being with him again—in every way—simply felt...good.

She liked his family, too. Which was a good thing, because, if she moved there, they'd be living together. In the same house. She had reservations about that, too.

How much privacy could there be with that many people sharing a home? They'd be bumping into each other all the time. And how would she keep an entire ranch house sanitized if Emma got sick again?

Even worse, what if they did move to Butter-scotch Ridge and Emma loved it…but things didn't work out between Lizzie and Danny? Her heart clenched. What then?

But she knew. Some part of her brain had already worked it out. As she had for the last five years, Lizzie knew it was just smart to always have a plan B. As much as she didn't want to need one, she had to have one.

With a start, she realized that Danny was still waiting for her answer. They all were.

"Well?" he asked, a little breathlessly.

"I… Can we talk about this in private?"

His shoulders drooped. "Sure." Of unspoken accord, they turned to her room in tandem.

"Seriously?" Sam muttered.

Mark chuckled. "What is this privacy of which you speak?"

"Leave them be. Let them talk," Luke said.

But once she and Danny were alone in her room, she didn't know what to say.

He cleared his throat. "I'm sorry I didn't mention this before. It's just that, well, things have been…"

"I know. I know. It just…surprised me. That's all."

"I'm sorry about that. But I really would like you to come. Please?"

All the possibilities, all the potentialities flooded her mind. They weren't all great, but Lizzie knew that if she and Danny were ever to be together again, she had to give him a real chance. Living five hours apart was not a real chance.

She glanced at him, staring at her, waiting. Perhaps holding his breath. It wasn't fair for her to keep him dangling when she knew her answer. Whether he'd like it or not, well, that was to be seen.

"You realize that's not going to be possible for at least six months." Even though Emma was doing well, she needed to be close to the hospital for daily and weekly tests, even after she'd been released.

He raked his hair. "Yeah. Yeah, I do. I just… Well, I'd like something to look forward to, you know? I'm going to have to go back to the ranch soon." When she didn't respond, he cleared his throat and said, "Will you and Emma come? Once the doctors say it's okay?" His expression was sincere.

"All right," she said, her tone somber. "Emma and I will come for a visit."

"A visit?"

"You know. To see how it goes." Lizzie hated the wounded expression on Danny's face. "You know. Take it slow." And when he didn't respond, "I—we—have Emma to think of. We have to consider what's right for *her*—"

"She's going to love it there. You both will. And we will do everything we can to make it as safe as possible for her. I promise."

"You can't promise something like that."

He took her face in his hands. "I can. I do." He

lowered his head and kissed her gently. His lips quirked against hers. "How long is a visit, anyway?" he murmured.

She chuckled. "We'll see."

"I can't wait," Danny said, wrapping his arm around her shoulders. He kissed her on the temple.

"Me, either." Lizzie smiled up at him. Yes. Once Emma's doctors said it was safe for her, they would try it, living on the ranch. With Danny. And his family.

But if things didn't work out, it wasn't like they had nowhere to go. Nan would always welcome them back.

If things didn't work out, there was always a plan B.

"Are you sure you're okay with this?" Danny asked later that night as he held her in the afterglow of their quiet lovemaking.

"Hmm?" Her brain hadn't returned yet.

"With moving… I mean, *visiting* the ranch once Emma's got the doctor's approval?"

"Sure, I'm okay with it." She nuzzled closer. "I do think it would be great for Emma."

He bit his lip. "Yeah. Great for Emma. But what about you? Your job? Your life here?"

"I can work remotely. I've been doing it for so long it shouldn't be a problem. Emma's my life, other than Nan, but she'll be fine without us."

He swallowed. Heavily. Then cleared his throat. "So you don't mind moving to the boondocks?"

"Visiting," she reminded him with a smile.

"Visiting. You don't mind?"

She didn't dare tell him she was looking forward to it. Excited about it, even. "You seemed to adjust to the country, and you're a Vegas boy. Maybe I can, too?"

"Then why are you so worried?"

She frowned at him. "What makes you think I'm worried?"

He levered up and gazed down at her. "Because you're *visiting*. In case it doesn't work out. If you think both you and Emma will love it…why would it not work out?"

Heat crawled up her cheeks. Well, crap. She hadn't wanted to go there. But maybe it was better if she did. Take a page out of Sam's book and just throw it out there in a big sloppy mess. "Okay. What if…*we* don't make it?"

His eyes widened, as though he'd never even contemplated such a thing. "Why wouldn't we make it? We're both Emma's parents. Look at how we found each other again, after everything that happened between us. And this…" He waved at the sheets tangled on the bed. "This is pretty freaking awesome, too."

"But we didn't make it the last time." It hurt to remind him, but it was true.

He paled. A muscle in his cheek flexed. "We

were different people then. I've changed. You've changed. Lizzie, we can make it work. I promise."

She sighed as she leaned up to kiss him. "We'll see."

"We'll see?" His expression tightened. "Lizzie, do you know what it did to me when you left? How it crushed me?"

"I had to go. You know why."

He shook his head brusquely. "That's not what I'm talking about. I…" He took a deep breath, as though preparing to reveal the dark well of his soul. "I never forgot you, Lizzie. Never stopped thinking about you. Never even looked at another woman. I couldn't."

Her pulse thudded at his confession. It broke her heart, but warmed her at the same time.

"Did you…?" He paused.

"Did I what?"

"Were there other men for you?"

Was he kidding? She was a single mother with a full-time job. "No." Her response was on a laugh.

He peeped at her. "Not even… Dr. Blake?"

Oh, good glory. "Not even him," she said.

Tension left him. "Good." He smiled crookedly and pulled her close once more. He made love to her again, and she enjoyed it, but she didn't miss the silent desperation in his attempt to show her that this, the passion they shared, was worth the risk.

It was a valiant effort on his part, but she wasn't fooled into abandoning her prudence. After the last five years, restraint was too deeply ingrained in the fiber of her being. Being cautious was who she was now, and being cautious around a man who could cause her so much pain was only practical.

Danny wasn't thrilled with Lizzie's hesitation. He'd been hoping for a little more enthusiasm. He lay awake most of the night trying to think up clever plans to win her heart, but most of them were inadequate.

The next morning, after the family had left, he and Lizzie went together to the hospital to tell Emma the news. He hoped her reaction to the prospect of coming to Butterscotch Ridge was more enthusiastic than her mother's.

To be fair, he understood Lizzie's concerns. How could he not? And, hell, he had plenty of concerns of his own, given his own terrible upbringing. What if he did something horribly wrong? What if he hurt Emma the way his mother had hurt him? Or worse, the way his father had?

Though he tried to be the best dad he could with Emma, there was always that little voice in the back of his head, reminding him how bad some parents could be. Reminding him of the role models he'd had—or rather, not had. He worried that someday, such ugliness could come from him, though he couldn't imagine himself ever savaging her piggy bank for drug money, or leaving her alone in the house with nothing to eat for three days while he partied with a new lover. He couldn't imagine denying her existence, either, as his father had done, or refusing to help his child's mother in the most basic of ways.

As he always did, he stuffed such fears away. Out of sight, out of mind. He wanted more than anything to be a good father to his child. A *great* father. All he needed was the chance.

He wasn't sure what he'd do if Emma didn't want to move to the country. Or visit. He couldn't move here. Not until he'd fulfilled his promise to work the ranch for three years.

So he worried about what Emma would say and what the doctors would say all the way to the hospital. Lizzie must have been thinking about that, too, because neither of them spoke much on the short trip.

Emma was on her bed, wearing her thinking tiara and working a puzzle, when they walked into her room. "Hey, sweetie," Lizzie said, giving her a kiss. "Did you have a good night?"

"Yep," Emma said, holding up a half-finished maze. "Look."

"Nice. What'd you have for breakfast?" She lifted the dome on the bedside tray and sniffed.

"Waffles. They were good." She shot a look at her mom. Her brow wrinkled. She frowned. "What is it?"

Lizzie jerked upright. The dome clanged back down. "What? What makes you think there's an *it*?"

Emma flopped back on the pillows and sighed. "*Mommy.* You know I can tell. You get the *face.*"

"The *face*?" Lizzie grimaced. "I have a *face*?"

"It's your bad-news face."

Danny frowned at Lizzie. "Is that your bad-news face?" He put his hands on his hips and asked, "Why is *this* bad news?"

"This is not my bad-news face. This is my good-news face." She forced a grin and showed it to Emma.

"It is good news, Emma, honey." Danny sat down next to her and took her hand. "When you get all better, and the doctors say it's safe, I'd like for you and your mom to come stay at the ranch for a while." He was very careful not to use the words *visit* or *move*, because apparently they hit tender spots with Lizzie. "Are you okay with that?"

Emma stared at him. "Stay? At. The. Ranch?" She huffed each word on a breath. Her eyes sparkled and her wispy hair trembled.

"Visit," said Lizzie.

Emma ignored her. "With Uncle Luke and Uncle Mark and Uncle DJ and Grandma Dorthea and Auntie Sam?"

Danny blinked. "Um, yes. And me, too, honey. I'll be there."

She squealed and bounced on the bed and nodded her head so hard, her tiara fell off. "We're going to live at the ranch with Luke!"

"Visit," Lizzie reiterated, but with a smile.

Danny grinned back.

Okay. Sure. Emma was excited to see *Luke*. But at least she hadn't refused.

It was tough for Danny to leave Emma and Lizzie to return to the ranch, but they understood he had made a commitment. The only reason he left was because Emma was doing so much better on her anti-rejection protocols. She still had at least another week in the hospital, and then another six months or so of testing until they could even consider a change of scenery. Thankfully, they weren't that far apart, and he knew he could come visit at any time.

Going back to Butterscotch Ridge and getting back into the routine on the ranch wasn't easy, either, but what was? He'd made a promise to his siblings, and to DJ in particular, and he fully intended to see it through.

At the start of all this, he never imagined he'd fit in with his siblings at all, not really, so it was surprising to find himself frequently embroiled in long discussions with DJ about philosophy and football, or raucous exchanges with Mark and Sam…even somewhat comfortable silences with Luke as they worked side by side.

Strange as it seemed, he started to feel at home there. Like he'd finally found a place he belonged. If only Emma and Lizzie were here, it would be perfect.

Each evening the siblings gathered after a hard day for a big family dinner and, when they weren't too tired, boisterous conversation and hilarious chatter, but for Danny, the bright moment in his day was when he could relax and talk to Emma and Lizzie.

He couldn't wait until they were here, with him. When he had time off, he spent it preparing the two rooms across the hall from his. There was an adjoining bathroom, so it would be perfect for Lizzie and Emma. More to the point, it would assure her she had her own space, so she wouldn't get spooked. A space she could sanitize to her heart's delight.

Danny's room was larger and had an en suite. He couldn't help thinking maybe, eventually, Lizzie would sleep here. With him.

How could she think they might not work out?

How could they not work out?

They were perfect together. And if they weren't, they could work on perfect. Life was a journey, right?

Meanwhile, his life consisted of sleep, food, work, repeat, so it was something of a thrill when Mark invited him over for dinner at his place one night. He appreciated Mark asking him over. Of all his siblings, he was the easiest to be around.

So at the end of the day's ride, Danny clapped off as much of the dust as he could, washed his hands and slicked back his hair, then made his way in the waning October sunlight to Mark's cabin—

one of the six built for crew with families, back by the bunkhouse.

A chorus of barks rose to greet him as he stepped onto the porch. Mark opened the door and the hounds rushed out. He'd already met them all, but Tallulah Bell gave him a crotch sniff just to be polite. His brother ushered him in. "Beer?"

"Sure." Danny let the dogs nuzzle his hand, because who wouldn't?

Mark made his way around a couple of yapping fur balls to the stove. "I made chili. I hope you like it."

"Love it."

"It's Grandma's recipe, so if you want it spicier, I have the goods." He pulled a tray out of the pantry with a selection of hot sauces.

"Oh, wow." Danny checked the labels and chuckled. If he ate that hot sauce, he'd be in a fetal position tomorrow. "I'm sure it's great the way it is."

While the chili finished simmering, Mark gave Danny a tour of his cabin, which was really much larger than it seemed. He had a living room and kitchen, a master bedroom with a private bathroom and another bedroom that he used for storage.

"Nice place," Danny said as the tour ended, back in the kitchen.

"Yep." Mark dropped into an overstuffed chair and gestured for Danny to do the same. "I think one of these places would be perfect if you and Lizzie decide not to stay in the big house. Besides, it'd be nice having neighbors."

Danny nodded, though he hadn't even thought that far ahead.

The conversation continued over dinner, which included a pretty damn good side of cornbread—Maria's recipe this time. And, of course, more beer. It was a pleasant discussion. Mark talked about the town, and the people Danny might meet if he stayed, and shared more stories about his childhood.

At one point, Mark sighed and said, "I've got to say, I'm sure glad you came along. It's nice having another brother."

"Thanks."

"I can't wait for Emma and Lizzie to get here. Everyone is so excited." He snorted a laugh. "Did you see what Luke is building next to the vegetable garden?"

"I saw he was doing something there. Some miniature house?"

"A rabbit hutch. He's determined to have it ready before Emma gets here. He's planning a swing set and a sandbox, too. Think he's excited?"

Danny grinned. "Maybe a little. It's going to be months, though."

"I know." Mark sighed. "But he loves that kid." Yeah. He did. "It's so cool the way he and Emma have bonded."

"Sure is," Danny said, ignoring that tiny prick of...was it jealousy? Of course she loved him. She *should* love Luke. He'd saved her life. Danny, on the other hand was...the sperm donor.

"I mean, after what he's been through... I can't even... Man. It's been a miracle for him. He's so much...happier."

Happier? *Happier than what?* Danny took a sip of beer. "Um, are we talking about the same Luke?"

Mark chuckled. "Yep. Believe it or not. I mean, he was always quiet and serious, even as a kid. But when he came back from Afghanistan, he was a completely different person. Bitter, wounded and lost. I think bonding with Emma is showing him the way back. That's what I mean by miracle. She needed him and he needed her. And they found each other at just the right time."

Well, that was good to know, that some kind of good had come out of Emma's illness. "Afghanistan couldn't have been a picnic."

"Not even. It was hell to begin with, and then Luke lost his best friend over there. To come back alone without him was really tough."

"I can imagine."

"It was an IED. Got them both."

Danny frowned. "The scar on his face?"

Mark nodded. "The one you can see, and the ones you can't. The bomb killed Brandon immediately, and hit Luke from the side. For a while, the doctors didn't think he'd even be able to walk again."

"He seems to walk just fine," Danny said. Luke was tough as nails. Or seemed like it.

"That's because he's stubborn and doesn't want anyone to know it still hurts like hell. But every once in a while, I can tell he's in pain."

"Huh."

The conversation sputtered like a wet candle for a minute and then Mark cleared his throat. "So…" he said. Danny glanced at him, snared by his odd tone more than anything else. He took a sip of his drink and then pinned Danny with a sharp gaze. "Lizzie? You two thinking about making it permanent?"

Something clogged his throat. He coughed. "What?"

"You know. Lizzie. You gonna marry her?"

Holy crap. What a question. Shards of panic sliced through him. Hadn't he just spent days thinking about his determination to be a family man—and the odds he was playing, given his history? "I…don't know."

Mark made a face. "Don't you? You have a daughter together—"

"Yeah, well, you and I both know that hardly requires marriage."

"And you're crazy about Emma."

Yes. True. But the idea of popping the question was…terrifying. What if she said no?

"Lizzie and I are, ahem, taking it slow. I mean, we only just reconnected a few months ago. And I didn't even know about Emma until then. We have to do this right, if we do it at all. Especially to make sure Emma is…you know…not hurt."

"Okay." Mark saluted him with his beer. "Just don't take too long. Lizzie's a beautiful woman and there are a lot of lonely men in these parts. Just sayin'."

Great. Just great.

Well, if nothing else, his conversation with Mark had given him a lot to think about.

Chapter Ten

To everyone's delight, the transplant team announced that Emma could go home in mid-December. Lizzie was over the moon. She'd spent the past month preparing for this day, and already had special air filters installed in the condo, purchased extra linens so she could change Emma's bed every day and fully researched an antimicrobial diet.

Even though Emma could now come home, there were still restrictions. One of the worst was that Lizzie had to limit her visitors. That meant she had to say no to the Stirlings, who wanted to come for Christmas.

Danny was there, though, watching Emma open

her—sanitized—presents on Christmas Eve. When Lizzie caught him wiping something from his eye, she asked if he was all right.

He shrugged. "Sure. I'm just enjoying Emma's excitement. We, ah, never had a Christmas like this when I was a kid," he said.

"No presents?" Emma stopped ripping paper and gaped at him.

He forced a smile. "No, sweetie. We didn't have money for presents back then." He glanced back at the table where they'd just had dinner. "No fancy dinner, either."

Emma tipped her head to the side. "What about pie?"

"Nope. Heck, I was happy with a bologna sandwich."

She came to his side. Patted his hand. "No presents. No pie. How sad."

He pulled her onto his lap with an exaggerated groan that was barely muffled through his mask. "Not really. You just do with what you have, honey. And then, when you do get pie, boy, you sure do appreciate it. It's real important to be thankful for what you have."

He glanced at Lizzie then, and a shiver walked through her. "Emma," she said, surely not to evade her emotions, which were always tender at this time of year. "I think there's a present for your dad under the tree. Why don't you find it?"

Naturally, she dived into the trove with alacrity,

quickly finding the box and carrying it to her father as though it were the gift of the Magi.

"For me?" he asked through a laugh. "What is it?"

Emma giggled. "You have to open it." And open it he did.

He did shed a tear then, as he sat there holding the mug that said World's Best Dad. But, of course, he denied it.

The next six months passed quickly. During that time, Danny visited nearly every weekend—except for a couple weeks in January because the passes closed down due to snow.

Lizzie was busy with work and running Emma to the hospital for blood draws and checkups. In early May, Emma's port was removed and restrictions were decreased, including the requirement for constant mask wearing at home, though it was still recommended if Emma was out in public.

In June, Dr. Blake broke the wonderful news that Emma was cleared to visit her dad in eastern Washington.

The closer the day came, the more excited Emma was to see her daddy, her aunt and uncles…and the ranch.

Emma helped Lizzie pack by bouncing on the bed among the folded underwear and singing her new song titled, "I'm gonna go see Uncle Luke," which she belted incessantly into her microphone hand.

"You're going to see your daddy, too," Lizzie reminded her, more often than she should have to.

"Oh, I know, Mommy. But he's my dad. He will always be there for me."

Lizzie blinked and stared at her daughter. "What? Where did you hear that?"

Emma made big eyes. "Because he told me, silly."

"He told you he would always be there for you?" Something lodged in her throat.

"Of course he did."

Of course he did.

She had to turn away. To hide her smile. Her heart blossomed. What a good father Danny had turned out to be. She'd done the right thing, bringing him into their lives. She'd have to tell him again when he came to pick them up.

When Danny and Mark finally arrived to help with the move, it was almost surreal.

This was it.

This was the first day of a new life.

The guys filled Lizzie's car with clothes and toys and books, and strapped the few pieces of furniture she'd decided to take to Mark's truck. Fortunately, they didn't have a lot of stuff, so they hadn't needed a mover.

Nan went with Lizzie and Emma down to the garage to see them off. "Now I can finally make a mess," she said with a wobbly grin as they held each other tightly. Nan discreetly wiped her eyes before hugging Emma, telling her to *be good...but not too good.*

"Come visit soon," Lizzie charged her, with another tearful hug.

"I will," Nan responded. "You can't get rid of me this easily."

Of course, they both laughed at that, which led to even more sniffling and hugging before Lizzie finally put herself into the car, though she stared back at her sister, and waved, until she disappeared from view.

Oh, it was hard leaving Nan. She'd been a bulwark in their lives for six long years. And they hadn't been easy years. First there had been Lizzie's worries about her pregnancy. Then, how to raise a daughter, and then, the nightmare of Emma's illness.

But now, everything had changed. All Lizzie's former worries seemed to be resolved, or nearly. Her daughter was getting better and now, she and Emma and Danny were going to be together. Things were good now, Lizzie realized it might take a while to brush off the constant stress of five years, but she was determined to try.

It was a long drive from Seattle to Butterscotch Ridge, but not boring. Emma did puzzles and sang and waved at Mark whenever they happened to pass each other on the road. Danny drove Lizzie's car, and he and Lizzie chatted as she enjoyed the passing greenery...until they crossed the mountains and hit the wide-open plains. Not much green in those grand vistas; the blue bowl of the sky arched, unimpeded, over their heads.

In the far distance, she saw a thunderstorm— big gray clouds with silver streams of rain pouring down—but it could have been a hundred miles away for all she knew. With no trees or mountains, you could see forever.

Though they arrived in Butterscotch Ridge in the early evening, the sun was still high in the summer sky, allowing Lizzie to take full stock of surrounding landscape. Though there was a lot of brown—butterscotch brown—it had a certain stark beauty. When Danny turned off the highway and they passed beneath a huge sign emblazoned with the words *Stirling Ranch*, Lizzie's pulse started to pound. Her mouth went dry.

"You're gonna start seeing the house after we round this ridge," he said.

What? "Wait, *start* seeing it?" Lizzie asked.

"Mmm-hmm." He nodded. "It's, ah, something."

Emma popped up between them and said, "What's something?"

Lizzie frowned at her. "Get your seat belt back on, young lady."

"But we're almost there."

Lizzie almost responded, *"And most fatalities occur within five miles of the home,"* but simply said, "Sit," until Emma did with a theatrical moan.

"And your seat belt." She glared until she heard

a click. And then she whipped around with a sigh. And, yes, she caught Danny's grin.

"You're pretty good at that," he said.

"Yeah?" she muttered. "Just wait." She was about to say more, but they took that turn and there it was. The *house*.

Her heart stuttered. "Danny, it's huge."

He shrugged. "You get used to it. The three of us have our rooms in one wing—"

"Wing?"

"So we'll be close, but you and, um, Emma will still have privacy." Lizzie noticed a little hesitation in his words. She wondered just how much separation he wanted from them, but shook off the thought as they pulled up in front of the house.

Good glory. She'd imagined they'd all be sharing a large farmhouse or something…but this?

There was no time to ponder things as Danny hopped out, ran around to take her hand, and then Emma's, and led them up the steps, across the porch and into the house.

Sam was there to greet them with a hug.

"We beat Mark," Emma said in a rush.

"I can see that you did." Sam winked at Danny. "Good job."

He gave her a sharp salute.

"Welcome." Sam ushered them into the grand foyer.

Lizzie had expected a beautiful home, but not this. Between the curving staircase, shiny wooden floors and a chandelier—an actual chandelier—it was hard not to gape. "Come along, Emma," she said, because her daughter *was* gaping, standing there beneath the crystal behemoth with her mouth open and twirling so she could watch it catch the light.

Sam grinned. "Emma, Grandma's excited to meet you." She led them into a comfortable sitting room on the left side of the foyer. The portrait of an old man—Daniel Senior? Lizzie guessed—hung in a place of prominence above the mantel. There were other pictures scattered around; one of a beautiful woman done up in black and white caught her eye. "That's our mom," Sam said. "She died when we were little. This one over here is our dad." She handed the picture to Lizzie and her heart did a little flip. Wow. He looked a lot like Danny.

"They're here, Grandma," Sam said to the older woman napping upright on the divan with a cup of tea in her hand. She opened her eyes and set the teacup on the table, then turned to survey her company. She appeared to be a frail old woman with a wisp of silver hair, a cane by her side and a touch of a tremor, but her eyes were bright and blue and full of mischief. When she spotted Emma, she smiled widely and touched her hands to her rouged cheeks. "And who is this darling?" she cooed as she gestured for Emma to come closer.

"I'm Emma," she said.

"Aren't you adorable?" Dorthea took her hands.

"You know, I had a blue dress just like that when I was little."

"Really? This one is my favorite!"

Dorthea laughed. "Oh, she's charming. So charming." Her gesture embraced them all as she motioned to the chairs like a grand hostess of old. "Sit. Sit. Shall we have some tea?" And then, before anyone could respond, "Sam, go fetch more tea. Cookies, too, will you? I'm peckish." And then, to Emma, "I hope you like cookies."

Sam rolled her eyes, but did so, returning quickly with a fresh pot of tea and plates of cookies—which made Emma lick her lips.

As they nibbled and chatted, Luke and DJ, hair freshly slicked down after a quick shower, joined them. Emma gave a whoop, of course, and ran into Luke's arms. He twirled her around and loudly smooched her cheek. When he sat, he held Emma on his lap. "I'm so glad to see you're better, Emma Jean," he said in a gruff voice.

"I'm glad to be better, Uncle Luke."

And everyone laughed. From joy, perhaps.

Lizzie sighed. The *feeling* so very much reminded her of the nights they'd all stayed up and talked when the family had come to visit. It was nice, comfortable and...it felt like home.

She'd never had so much support, so many people who cared for her and Emma. Now, she had Danny, and Emma had a plethora of uncles and aunts.

Wow. They had a whole new way of life to get used to. If, of course, everything worked out. If, of course, they stayed.

Though the house was larger than Lizzie had imagined, it still felt welcoming and warm. The kitchen and family rooms were on the main floor, and the second floor was all bedrooms. Lizzie quickly realized her fears about privacy had been utterly unfounded. Danny hadn't been kidding when he said they had their own wing. It was at the far end of the second floor, right off the main hall in the back.

Sam was excited to show Lizzie and Emma their bedrooms, which adjoined through the bathroom on one side of the hall. Lizzie's room was nice. Roomy and comfortable with a large window seat. The sea foam walls were exactly her taste, as was the quilted duvet in complimentary colors. The flowers on her bedside table were a lovely touch, as well.

As she passed through the bathroom to check out Emma's new digs—with hand-painted bunnies frolicking on the walls—Lizzie couldn't help catching a whiff of...was that bleach?

Oh. It was. Her heart lifted.

Bleach meant things were clean. Bleach meant rooms were disinfected. Bleach meant it was safe.

Beyond that, it meant that someone had cared enough to think of Emma, and to make an extra effort to ensure her room was as hygienic as possible. She also noticed that there was a bottle of sanitizer on each bedside table, and one in the bathroom. Even though Emma was better, such efforts were heartily appreciated. They weren't entirely in the clear yet.

"You okay?" Danny whispered in her ear.

She smiled at him. "Yeah. Sure. It's just...very nice."

Was it her imagination, or did his shoulders slump a little in relief? "Awesome. And, just so you know, everyone has agreed to hose down in the stable bathroom before coming into the house."

"Hose down?" She chuckled.

"Yeah, you know. Kick off our boots. Change clothes. Shower. Put whatever we were wearing in the laundry when we get into the house. That sort of thing. Ranching is pretty dirty work. We know Emma needs a super clean environment for the next year or so."

Something swelled in her chest. Something painful and beautiful. "Perfect. Thank you." She kissed his cheek. He turned her head to kiss her lips. It wasn't until Emma started making hacking noises that she finally pulled away, but with a grin.

"Let's see your room, mister," she said.

"Right this way." He led them through the double doors to his chamber.

And wow. Danny's room was *huge*. It had a large sitting area with overstuffed and embroidered chairs in front of the fireplace, an enormous four-poster bed, a grand bathroom and closets for days.

"Seriously?" Lizzie sent him a joking side-eye. "*This* is your room?"

He checked to make sure Emma was still preoccupied with Sam in her own room before he leaned in and whispered, "It could be your room, too. You know. If you want."

If you want?

A sizzle licked through her and she looked away, but only because she needed to focus and he was distracting. "We need to talk about that."

"Talk about what?" He nibbled on her neck. Shivers cascaded through her.

"Talk about...*you know.*"

"Mmm."

She yanked away, because his nibbles were starting to fray her concentration. "How are we going to handle this?"

His grin was annoyingly confident. The cowboy scruff around it was just annoying. "I figured we'd just wait 'til she falls asleep."

"That's crazy." *Might work.*

"All we have to do is make sure you're back in your bed before Emma wakes up."

That should be no problem. Lizzie had always been an early riser. Even in the days when sleep had been a luxury. "All right. Once Emma's settled in here, that's what we'll do."

He ignored her qualification and pulled her into a spin. "That's what we'll do."

"What's what you'll do?" Emma said, pulling Sam by the hand from her own room.

"Hey, honey," Danny said, going down on one knee. "What do you think of your new room?"

She nodded. "I like it."

"Great. And...what do you think of your great-grandmother?"

Emma shrugged. "Nice."

"Emma's never had a grandmother, much less a *great* grandmother," Lizzie added.

"Oh, well, now you do," Sam said.

"She's nice," Emma said. "She smells like flowers."

Sam chuckled. "Yes. She does. That's the soap she uses. I bet if your mom says it is okay she'll let you try it." Sam sighed and gave Emma another hug. "Gosh, we're all so happy you came."

Emma grinned with a delight Lizzie hadn't seen in a long while. "I'm happy, too," she said as she returned Sam's hug. "I like having a big family."

Lizzie leaned against Danny, reveling in the warmth of his arm around her. He looked down at her and smiled. And, for the moment, everything was perfect.

Danny was amused that Emma and Lizzie's first dinner at the ranch was like a fancy party—very much unlike the workday dinners where they all tromped in, exhausted, and ate in relative silence.

But tonight, as everyone headed into the dining room, the atmosphere was so festive it felt like a party. And why not? Lizzie and Emma were here. Danny felt like celebrating, as well.

When Lizzie had walked back into his life—was it almost ten months ago?—he could never have imagined this change of events, never dreamed he could be so happy. So fulfilled. But then, to be honest, back then, he hadn't felt worthy of such blessings.

Well, he felt worthy now. He felt capable now and confident that he did, indeed, have something of value to offer his child. He just didn't know if Lizzie saw it that way. He vowed to show her in whatever way he could.

Could she ever overlook what an idiot he'd been before he'd come here? Before he'd grown up?

He hoped so.

As they took their seats around the dinner table, Dorthea insisted that Danny sit on one side of her and Emma sit on the other. As these were places of prominence, at least for a five-year-old, Emma was pleased. But she insisted Luke sit next to her, and for once, he seemed content to be commanded.

He and Emma put their heads together and talked while the conversation carried on around them as Sam and Mark brought out the food.

Throughout the meal, his grandmother made it

a point to entertain him, launching into a series of stories about her late son—his prodigal father—and her husband, who had so recently passed away. The stories were mostly funny, but they made Danny a little sad because he'd never met either of the men. As much as he realized he was grateful to have found the Stirlings, he couldn't help but feel a sense of loss for the connection he'd missed out on with his father. And his grandfather, too.

He stabbed a piece of meat with his fork and pushed down the emotion. Why lament the past when the present was so good?

By dessert, everyone was telling stories about their childhood and what it was like growing up on the ranch, joking with Emma about how she'd be a cowgirl in no time.

Emma, who'd been excited to begin with, picked up on their energy. With that—and a very sweet dessert of cake and ice cream—she fairly hummed with it. Since Lizzie had insisted on limiting her sugar intake during her six month recuperation, this sudden influx was particularly potent. Her voice became louder and her laugh more forced. She interrupted people and ignored Lizzie's gentle admonitions to be polite. It was Danny's first experience with an overstimulated child, and it was an eye-opener.

"Now you see why she doesn't get ice cream every night," Lizzie said in an undertone.

"Yeah," he said. "Good idea."

When Emma suddenly yawned, Lizzie began trying to suggest it was time for bed. Luckily, she had some help.

"Oh, you must be tired," Mark said, noticing Lizzie's struggle with the little girl.

He noticed a lot of things, Danny found. "It's been a long day for all of us," he said, slipping his arm around Lizzie. "You ready to turn in?" He caught a sudden glimmer in her eye, and an answering thrill rolled through him like thunder, but he forced himself to ignore it. He'd resolved himself to give Lizzie all the space she needed to get used to the place…and the idea of staying.

"We probably should," Lizzie said on a sigh. "Come on, honey. Bedtime."

Emma looked horrified. "But Mommy…"

Danny cleared his throat. He was kind of new at this parenting game, but he knew enough to back Lizzie up. "You heard your mom. Time for bed, Emma."

She stilled. Met his gaze with one of her own. Yeah, he was new at this game, but he could recognize a rebellion when he saw it. So he added, "We need to get a lot of sleep if we're going to explore the ranch tomorrow."

He was pretty sure she was trying to decide how serious he really was. She must have decided he was indeed serious because she sighed heavily, then turned to Luke and said, "Sorry. I gotta go now. I'll see you tomorrow?"

Luke grinned. "Okay, kiddo."

"'Night, Emma," everyone chorused.

And as he and Lizzie followed Emma back to their rooms, Lizzie leaned over and murmured to Danny, "Pretty good. For a beginner." And then she winked.

Storytime was difficult for Lizzie that night. For one thing, Emma really was hyper, and for another, there was Danny, on the other side of her, long and lean, tan and warm, reading *Mrs. Piggle-Wiggle* like a sexy children's-book model or something. It was hard for Lizzie to focus.

Then, after they suffered the ubiquitous barrage of "one more chapter," they tucked Emma in, kissed her good-night and turned out the light.

As he walked her down the hall to her door, Danny whispered, "If you want, you can come over to my room when she's asleep." Lizzie's heart did a little flip-flop. "We can...talk."

Talk? "Mmm," she murmured, in an effort to remain blasé.

"Is that a yes?"

She narrowed her eyes at him. "We'll see." Then she pushed him back toward his own room. "Good night," she said in a louder voice for Emma's benefit, then closed her door on his too-handsome face.

As much as she wanted to go to his room and... talk, she was torn. This was Emma's first night in a new room, a new house, a new environment.

Shouldn't Lizzie be here in case she woke up and was frightened? Of course she should.

With a huff, she relaxed on the bed and picked up the book on her night table. She flipped to her bookmark and began to read.

But it had been so long since she and Danny had been together. *Really* together. Alone. And while she'd always considered herself a logic-driven woman, she couldn't deny that since they'd reunited in *that* way, she'd gone through some great awakening, like a cocoon opening up to release a beautiful butterfly.

A horny butterfly.

It was all she could think about sometimes, being with him like that. And when she thought of it, her body reacted. Warming, melting, aching. At one point today, when she'd been loading the truck, a box had grazed her breast. The arousal had been so intense, she'd nearly dissolved right there.

She didn't remember being quite this voracious back in Vegas—and that was saying something.

Maybe it wouldn't be so bad to just pop over to Danny's room. Maybe they could just have a quick…chat, and then she could nip right back when they were through. That would work.

But what would she say if Emma woke up while she was gone? Or—*egads*—what if she walked in on them? She sighed. No. She wasn't going over to Danny's room. Not tonight, anyway.

She turned back to her book.

But what was the chance Emma would wake up? She rarely did at home. And Lizzie wouldn't be gone long, right?

In a rush, she got up and tiptoed through the bathroom to peek in on Emma. She was asleep, on her back with her arms splayed out, her mouth open wide. A gentle snore rose, and with it, a tingle in Lizzie's gut.

With extreme stealth, she closed Emma's door, tiptoed back to her own room and closed that door, as well. Then she made her way across the hall.

The second she tapped on his door, it opened and a large hand shot out and pulled her inside.

"What took so long? Is everything okay with Emma? Did she fall asleep in the new bed or was she too nervous? What about—?"

"Danny! Emma's fine. I promise." While she knew they were both thinking about, well, other things, it was clear that he also had their daughter's comfort in mind. He really was growing into fatherhood, more and more every day. "Does this door lock?" He showed her that it did. "We have to make this quick," she said. "I have to get back in case she wakes up."

"Quick?" He put out a lip. "I wasn't planning on quick."

"Well, it's quick or nothing, buddy," she said, using her body to back him toward the bed. She stalled when she saw he'd sprinkled rose petals in the shape of a heart on the duvet. "Oh! How lovely."

"Do you like it?" He lifted her and laid her into the petals.

"It smells wonderful. Thank you."

"My pleasure." He eased her back and hovered over her, his heat searing her.

"Where did you get them?"

He leaned down and kissed her neck. A warm, wet shiver rocked her. "In the garden. Don't tell Dorthea."

She returned the gesture, nuzzling his neck, as well. It was only good manners. Besides, she wanted to taste him. And, yes, his skin was smooth and warm, and his scent intoxicated her. His fingers closed on her breast, and she caught her breath as she waited, suspended, for him to find that tender bundle of aching nerves at its crest. When he touched her there, it was like a live wire. She couldn't hold back her moan. He responded by taking her mouth in another kiss.

Determinedly, he stripped away her clothes, piece by piece, until she was bare before him. And then he stilled. Stared. "God, you're beautiful." He caressed her body with a soft touch that made her shiver.

"Danny," she sighed as she opened her arms to him.

He quickly undressed, then came down at her side and kissed her breast, in a teasing tormenting way, as he stroked the other.

"You're going to make me crazy," she sighed.

He merely chuckled and kept on circling her nipple with that damned finger.

She decided to turn the tables, and levered over him, straddling him with her body. His hard length thrummed against her cleft, sending shivers through her. But she didn't allow herself to be deterred. She alternately teased his nipples and rubbed against his arousal, being very careful not to allow him too much pleasure, even though it drove her mad, as well.

Fortunately, Danny was an impatient man. With a growl, he rolled her over and pinned her down. "Oh, Lizzie." He kissed her deeply as he nudged against her aching core.

Her pulse pounded…more than usual. There was just something exhilarating about being together this way, knowing that at any moment they could be caught. Sure, the door was locked, but even hearing a knock would be a disaster. Especially now.

"Hurry," she whispered. "Hurry."

To her chagrin, Danny shifted his weight, and made his way down her body, nibbling and nipping here and there, stroking her in tender spots all the while.

Yes, she was in a hurry. Yes, she'd planned to do this in a rush. But knowing where he was headed, she couldn't bring herself to stop him. If there was one thing Danny did well, it was worship a woman.

And, ah. When he found her… His breath skated over her super-sensitized nerves as he tasted her.

The simple swipe of his tongue made her head spin, made her belly lurch. She arched into him with a groan.

Her body sang as the tension in her rose. Her heart thudded and she struggled for breath. "D-Danny…" she burbled as she felt the start of something glorious lift her. "Now."

Thank God, he was listening, that some part of his brain was still engaged. He moved up between her legs and guided himself into her. He filled her completely, seating himself deep within her with a sigh.

She could have stayed like that forever, except they both wanted more, needed more. He gave it to her like a beast, claiming her with hard hot strokes, each one driving her deeper into bliss. She could feel it, could tell when he came close to release. His body tightened like a bowstring and his lunges became more and more frenzied.

She didn't care. The delight that had been stalking her blossomed with a mind-boggling intensity, and then crashed over her like a wave of refreshing warm sea water on a Caribbean beach.

Danny crested, too, crying out her name and arching over her.

He collapsed, gasping, and then, after a while, when his breathing was nearly normal again, he leaned over and framed her face in his hands and kissed her. "Lizzie." A whisper.

Then, when she tried to leave the bed, to go back

to her room, he pulled her closer and murmured, "Stay awhile."

And she did.

Because this nest was too delicious to leave just now.

Chapter Eleven

Lizzie rolled over and cuddled closer to the hard warmth next to her. It was nice warmth. Smelled good. Her questing hand encountered smooth skin and followed it down Danny's chest until she found his stirring member.

"Mmm." His response was a sleepy mumble.

She smiled. She liked waking up in his bed. It was—

And then it hit her. *Crap!*

She'd slept here. *All night.*

She bolted upright, rummaged around for her clothes, and—damn it all, anyway—ran as fast as she could back to her room and collapsed on the bed, her heart pounding.

Thank heaven Emma wasn't up yet.

She really had to be more careful. How on earth would she explain *this* to a five-year-old?

She probably would have to explain...*something*, if this continued. But she didn't need to have that conversation with Emma today.

With a sigh, she stood, adjusted her blouse and knocked on Emma's adjoining door. There was no response, so she knocked again, then opened the door...to an empty room.

Emma wasn't there.

Her pulse stuttered. Panic flared.

Emma wasn't there. Where was she?

She whirled into Danny's room and caught him putting on a shirt. His back muscles rippled. She nearly lost her train of thought as something primal within her roared. With effort, she wrenched her attention away from that panoply of perfection. "We have to find Emma. She's not in her room."

Danny grinned and kissed her on the forehead. "She's probably out playing."

Lizzie shook her head, trying to get control of her panic. "She never gets up without me. She always comes and wakes me up." Yes, she knew she sounded hysterical. She felt hysterical. Emma had never done something like this before. Never done anything without telling Lizzie what she was up to.

"All right. Calm down. Why don't we go find her together?"

Lizzie nodded and cuddled against him. He put

his arm around her shoulder as they headed for the stairs. "This house is just so big," she said in a wail as they rounded another corner.

"I know." He gave her a squeeze as they came down the stairs and headed for the kitchen. "Mark lives in one of the smaller cabins."

"Cabins?" She glanced up at him as they walked.

"Yeah. A little farther out on the property. For crew members with family. They're nice." Was that a hopeful glance?

She couldn't dwell on interpreting his intentions at the moment. She was too—

Her lungs locked as she spotted Emma wearing her bunny ears, on her knees on a kitchen chair so she could lean closer to Luke across the table. The two were engaged in a deep conversation.

Oh, thank God. "Emma!" she cried, in too high a pitch apparently, because her daughter's head swiveled and her eyes widened with a look that said, *"What'd I do?"*

"Emma," she repeated in a calmer tone. "Good morning. I, ah…" Her gaze landed on Emma's outfit. "You dressed yourself! Oh, honey." Nothing matched, of course, but it made Lizzie smile.

Emma beamed with pride. "Yup. I'm getting all grown-up." Something in Lizzie's chest pinged. "You see? I can do things for myself."

Yes. She could. But it was so hard for Lizzie to let go of the precautions she'd had to take for over two years—to keep her daughter alive. And now, thanks to Luke, Emma's body could create her own protection from nearly every germ she encountered. But surely, she still needed her mother. Didn't she?

"You *are* doing great, Emma," Danny said, sliding into the chair beside her. "But we're still being careful. Right?"

As Emma nodded, her bunny ears flopped.

"I think your mom may be a little worried, though." Emma peeped at her over his shoulder. "I think she's worried that we, all three of us, have a lot to learn about living on a farm."

"Ranch," Luke amended.

"There's lots of machines and animals. Some dangerous stuff. Lots of new things to learn about safety."

Lizzie nodded. "I was terrified when you weren't in your room. You've never gone off without me before."

Emma pouted. "I came down here to see Uncle Luke."

"Yes. Yes. That's fine, honey. We'd just feel better if you check in with us before you do things. Just until we all get used to living here. Okay?" Hopefully that didn't come out as too controlling, but God only knew what kind of ideas a curious child could come up with on a ranch. And Emma had been sequestered for a huge chunk of her life. All she wanted to do was explore.

The thought made Lizzie's blood run cold. She knew she was overreacting. But would it be so terrible to be overprotective for a little while longer? She didn't want to smother her child, but a balance was hard to find sometimes.

Thankfully, Emma crossed her arms and issued a reluctant, "Okay, Mommy."

Relief coursed through her and she hugged her daughter. She knew that as time went on, Emma would demand more independence—which was as it should be. Lizzie would have to start learning to let go. Whether she wanted to or not.

After they all ate breakfast together, Luke took Emma to the barn to see the animals—masks on and no petting, per the doctor—as Danny and the others headed out to start on chores, which left Lizzie at a loose end.

Oh, sure, she could have gone to the barn, too, but she was filled with remorse about overreacting when Emma hadn't been in her room. She realized she needed to let go—a little, at least. Besides, Luke and Emma had a special bond she wanted to encourage.

It took a lot of self-discipline to let them have their time together, but her patience was challenged by the fact that she didn't have anything else to do. Other than her work and Emma, she hadn't had much else in her life. There hadn't been time for it.

And now that there was time…what was she to do with it? She had no idea.

She quickly discovered that if they were going to

stay here, she'd have to find a hobby, or go utterly insane. Eventually, she found herself on the porch, staring out at a beautiful summer day.

It was warm, but not too hot, and there was a pleasant breeze fluttering by. She sat on the swing, closed her eyes, dropped her head back onto a pillow and just listened. She could actually hear the wind here. It danced and rustled through the tall elms that shaded the yard. Oh, and the birdsong was lovely. That and the scent of newly mown hay. A cow lowed in the distance and somewhere a chicken squawked.

A smile curled on her lips. Not a lot of that in downtown Seattle, for sure.

As pleasant as it was, Lizzie wasn't used to lounging around in the sunshine—or being away from her daughter, which made her uneasy—so she headed out in search of Emma. She wasn't in the barn. She wasn't in the house. She wasn't in the yard.

Lizzie tried very hard not to panic, but the thought of tagging her daughter with GPS did flicker through her brain.

She finally heard an unmistakable laugh coming from the bunkhouse area, so she headed that way, trying to calm her heart by repeating the mantra *"it's going to be okay"* over and over again.

She spotted Mark in the distance and, as she came closer, she saw Emma standing at a large fenced-in area behind one of the cabins. And there, on the other side of the fence…puppies.

Now, it wasn't as though Lizzie disliked animals. She loved them. She really did. But animals were a high risk to children with suppressed immune systems. Lizzie had always kept Emma away from them.

And now, here she was, Lizzie's precious, fragile daughter, standing far too close to creatures that carried ticks and fleas and licked their butts and probably stepped in poop on a regular basis and tracked it everywhere they went.

Her first reaction was to scream something very parental and yank her daughter away. But she had overreacted this morning; she didn't want to do it again.

Besides, Emma was better, she reminded herself again. The doctors had been clear that she could engage in most normal activities, as long as she was careful to wash her hands and take other precautions. The fact that Emma was on one side of the fence and Mark and the dogs were on the other should calm her panic. Shouldn't it?

Beyond that, Emma was in awe. Lizzie had never seen her daughter so happy. Never.

"Look, Mommy!" she squealed. "Puppies."

Lizzie tried to hold back her smile in lieu of a stern glance, but she might have failed. "Adorable," she said, coming to Emma's side. Some of the older dogs trotted over to her and gave her a cursory sniff.

"Isn't she precious?" Emma pointed to the smallest puppy.

"Here," Mark said, handing Emma a dog treat. "Do you want to give her a cookie?"

Emma grinned as she negotiated the delicate transfer of biscuit from hand to snout through the chain link fence.

Lizzie forced her spine to relax. It really was a wonderful sight. She renewed her resolve to try to enjoy Emma's newfound freedom as much as everyone else did.

The delight on her daughter's face was precious. It was worth the battle to hold her tongue and not call warnings all the time. Maybe, after a while, she'd get used to it.

Still, the packet of antibiotic wipes in her pocket would come in handy when Emma was done here.

"So, you named her Daisy?" Mark asked.

"Yes. She looks like a Daisy, doesn't she, Mommy?"

Lizzie chuckled. "She sure does. How nice of Mark to let you name her."

Emma made a face. "Why wouldn't I name her?" she asked. "She's my dog."

"What?" Lizzie whipped her attention to Mark, who was watching Emma with hands on his hips and a grin on his face. When he saw Lizzie's expression, the grin faded.

"What?" he asked.

"You gave her a *dog*?"

"A puppy. Why not? I mean, the doctors said she was better, right?"

Oh, good glory. Who knew that having relatives could be so annoying? "You just don't give a little girl a puppy without asking her parents."

"Danny said it was okay."

Oh. Good. Glory.

"Where is he?" she fumed.

"Probably out in the back forty, fixing the fence with DJ." Mark grinned at her. "Listen, I had a puppy when I was Emma's age. It was a great experience. She'll learn how to take care of her, walk her, feed her… She'll learn responsibility, having a dog."

"But Daisy's staying here, right?" She gestured to the fenced area, which she now realized was a dog run.

"Sure, sure." Mark nodded and Lizzie exhaled. "For a few more weeks. And then, she'll move to the house."

"She'll sleep in my room, Mommy! Isn't that awesome?"

Not.

A volcano rumbled in Lizzie's gut. "Emma Jean. You know what the doctors said."

The pout meant she did.

Lizzie frowned at Mark. "Until she's one year out, no puppy."

"How long is that?" Mark asked.

To be safest? "December. *If*—and it's a big if—the doctor approves."

"But Mommy..."

"December. Emma! Remember what the doctor said. And Mark, don't forget to sanitize her hands when you're done!" With one more glare at Mark, Lizzie tromped back to the house where she could smolder in private.

She found a modicum of distraction from her annoyance in the library, scanning the book selection. Unfortunately, there were not many children's books. She'd have to do something about that if they stayed.

DJ poked his head in the door and stilled when he saw her. As though he'd been looking for her or something. "Hey, Lizzie," he said. "You a reader?" He gestured at the books.

She raised an eyebrow. "I read."

"Oh, great. These books were Grandpa's. He liked the classics. Said a good education was solid foundation for life. Made me read all of them."

She pulled out a copy of *For Whom the Bell Tolls* and opened the cover. The glorious scent of ink and must rose and she drew it in. She loved old books. Any books. And this one was a first edition. And signed. By Ernest Hemingway. What a treasure. She gently set it back in place. "I can see that. He had excellent taste."

"Yeah." DJ glanced around the room for a minute then said, "Ah, hey. Lizzie?"

"Mmm?"

"You said you're an accountant, right?"

"Yep. Seven years."

"Listen, ah… Could you take a look at something for me?"

What else did she have to do? "Sure."

Half an hour later, she realized she should have said no as she stared at the piles of files on DJ's desk. The ranch finances.

All of them.

They went back to the fifties.

DJ was prepping to have a company transfer everything into digital files and asked her if she would mind helping get things organized.

She'd said, "Of course," of course. She should have said no. This was *a lot* of work, but judging from the way DJ had skedaddled out of there as soon as she'd agreed, she'd figured out accounting wasn't his thing. Like, at all.

Ah, well. It would keep her busy, now that Emma didn't need her every moment of the day.

With a sigh, she dug in.

Danny found Lizzie in DJ's office surrounded by a mountain of paperwork. "Wow," he said as he kissed her. "What'cha doing?"

She made a face. "DJ asked me to go through the financial paperwork."

"Fun."

"Mmm." She cracked her neck and stood. "I'm cross-eyed."

"I thought you loved putting things in order." It was a joke, kind of.

She didn't appreciate it. "Luckily, your grandfather was a hoarder. He kept every receipt. Every one. At least that'll make things a little easier."

Danny grinned. "Where's Emma? I thought maybe the three of us could go on a walk. Explore a bit." He winked. "There's a pond not far—"

For some reason, Lizzie whirled on him. "Did you tell Mark he could give her a puppy?"

Uh-oh. It had seemed like a great idea at the time. Now, not so much. "One of his dogs had a litter. He's trying to place them."

"Well, why didn't you just ask for all of them?"

He blinked. "Because I thought we should start Emma off with one."

She stared at him and he suddenly realized her suggestion might have been sarcastic. Damn. He'd screwed up. This was all so new to him. He hated to think he'd blown it on the first day. "Hon, I'm sorry if I overstepped…"

She stilled, then shook her head. "No. You're her father. You didn't overstep so much as… How's this? Maybe, next time, we can talk about it first if it's something big like that?"

Heat walked up the back of his neck. He scrubbed at it. "Sure. Okay."

"The doctor said not for a year. Remember?"

"Of course. I just didn't realize Mark meant he wanted to give it to her *now*."

She sighed. "I'm sorry for snapping, Danny. This is just a lot for me to deal with…and not just moving to a ranch, you know?"

"I know." He wasn't sure he did, not really, but she seemed to need to hear that in the moment. He hugged her because she seemed to need that, too.

"I've had to protect her for so long from so much. And now… Now she… I just…"

"I know. I *know*." What a helpful phrase. Too bad this time, it set her off.

"No, Danny, you *don't* know. I spent years worried about every single move she made—even before she got sick. It was always me saying no, always me being the bad guy. And then *you* get to give her a puppy…" She took a deep breath. "Look. I know you meant well. I really do. But it's more important than ever to follow every single protocol every step of the way. The risk is too big."

"I'm really sorry, Lizzie. You're so right." He sighed heavily. "I have to be stronger—with her, everyone does. It's hard to say no when Mark wants to give her a puppy, Luke wants to give her a bunny, Sam wants to give her a pony—"

"Sam wants to give her a pony?"

"I told her no," he said quickly. "Point is, we're all adjusting."

"We are." She sighed and sent him a dark look. "Just know that when that puppy comes into the house, *you* are the one who's going to have to take care of it. It is not mine."

"It's Emma's puppy."

"Fine. Emma's puppy. But you take care of it when it cries all night or pees on the carpet, or barfs on the bed. Agreed?"

"I, ah, okay." It was probably the only answer. Definitely the right one, because she grunted and turned to make her way from the library out onto the porch.

Emma was on the lawn, watching Mark attempt to train her new puppy, so they sat on the swing, his arm around her and her head on his chest, and they watched as he tried to teach Daisy to sit. Daisy preferred to jump up and try to steal the treat he was offering.

Danny chuckled and held Lizzie closer.

How wonderful was this? Sitting here with Lizzie as the afternoon sun slanted through the trees. Sure, he was tired after a long day on the ranch, but it was a good tired, one his body was becoming used to. The work itself was invigorating and varied. He really enjoyed every day.

And now that Lizzie and Emma were here...he wanted *this* forever. He glanced at her, wondering how she felt about it. If this was as satisfying for her as it was for him, this kind of life. He wished he had the courage to just come out and ask her, but he knew he should probably wait.

It was definitely too soon to do something stupid like propose.

But, ah, that was what he wanted. He wanted—needed—her to be his. His wife. His.

Lizzie shifted. A sudden dampness touched his shoulder.

His breath froze. Aw, hell. Was she crying?

"Lizzie," he said, tipping her face up to his. "What is it?"

She stared at him, tears coursing down her cheeks. She shook her head and something in his chest clenched.

"Lizzie?" Did she really hate this place so much? Had he read everything wrong? Why was she crying?

"Oh, Danny." He hated that her voice wobbled. But then she smiled. A smile of gratitude that shone through her eyes and warmed his heart. "It's j-just so won-won-wonderful," she said through a sob. "Sitting here. Just wa-watching her pl-play."

Yes. It was. Wonderful.

So why did it make him wonder when the other shoe was going to drop?

Chapter Twelve

The next morning, after another night in Danny's arms, Lizzie headed to DJ's office to keep working on her project. She munched on Maria's delicious *mantecadas* and sipped rich coffee as she organized the financial documents. Things were starting to come together, but there were a few mysteries.

"How's it going?" a deep voice asked. She glanced up to see DJ had poked his head into the office. Just his head. Nothing else. In case the dark powers of accounting should suddenly try to suck him into the void. The guy must really hate paperwork.

"Good." She shot him a smile. "Slow, but good. I have to suspect your grandfather didn't like this end of the business, either."

Big, gruff DJ barked a laugh. "I s'pose not. To be honest, we're both the outdoorsy types. More at home on the back of a horse. This kind of stuff gives me the heebie-jeebies. But let me know if you need more help or explanations for stuff."

His grin was so engaging she had to respond in kind. "Okay. But I think I can figure most of it out. I mean, his notes are pretty good." Most of the time. Some of the regular payments in past years were well-documented. Some, however, were questionably vague. When she came across these, she set them aside. "There is something you could help me with…" She riffled through the piles until she found the file marked only, and mysteriously, *PD*. "Ah. This one."

DJ stepped into the room and took the sheaf of papers and flipped through them. His brow furrowed. "These go back twenty-five years."

Lizzie nodded. "Yeah. The large payments were issued on January first of each year, but I found a couple more, here and there, for different amounts." She shrugged. "No coding, so I have no idea what they were for. Any idea what PD stands for?"

DJ shook his head. "And this ain't chump change." He flipped through some more papers. "Huh."

"Find something?" Lizzie asked.

"Yeah. Looks like the last payment was made about a year ago. Just before Grandpa got sick."

"So whatever this payment was for, it wasn't paid this fiscal year."

"Right." Mark shook his head. "But we haven't had any bills or invoices for this amount."

"And there's no invoices or receipts in this file. Everything else has provenance."

"Just set it aside, I guess. We'll deal with it if it comes up."

"Okay." But even as Lizzie marked a fresh manila folder with the letters *PD*, she had to wonder what on earth this could be.

After DJ left, she was quickly reabsorbed into the project and worked clear through to lunch, when Sam came to drag her from her dungeon.

"You can't work all the time," she said.

Lizzie snorted and glanced at Sam's dusty jeans. "You do."

Sam grinned. "I *like* my work."

"Well, so do I."

"I don't see how anybody could like that," Sam said as they entered the kitchen, where the family usually ate their casual meals. Dorthea was there, sipping on tea. The empty soup bowl indicated she'd already eaten.

"Hello, Grandma," Sam said, giving her a kiss and easing a plate of biscuits closer.

Maria smiled at them. "What can I make you?" she asked.

"I can make lunch, Maria," Sam said, opening the fridge and staring into its depths. She sighed.

"How about a nice grilled cheese?" Maria suggested.

"Oh, yes. That would be perfect." Sam glanced at Lizzie. "How about you?"

"Grilled cheese sounds perfect."

Maria's eyes lit up. "There's some Beecher's cheese in there," she said. "Do you know it?"

Lizzie grinned. "I love Beecher's." It was a local brand, handmade in Seattle. She and Emma had once gone to the Pike Place Market to see it being made right there in the restaurant.

"Excellent." Sam grabbed a pan and started melting butter.

The smell made Lizzie's mouth water. She was hungrier than she'd thought.

"Crystal and Jack are coming over this afternoon," Sam said as she grated the cheese.

Lizzie smiled. She remembered Crystal from her visits to the B&G, but hadn't yet met her son. "That's great." It would be nice for Emma to make a friend.

"It'll be fun. Don't you think so, Grandma?"

Though Sam tried to engage her, Dorthea simply wasn't in the mood to chat today. In fact, she sat at the table, silent, and sipped her tea. Lizzie gave her a refill, but there was no response to that, either. But then her face suddenly broke into a wide grin.

Lizzie turned to see Emma, arms filled with weeds and wildflowers, clomp mud all over the wood floor as she entered the room through the back door. She headed straight to Dorthea and dumped the, ahem, bouquet in her lap, then said, "I smell food."

"Are you hungry, honey?" Lizzie asked. "We're having grilled cheese."

In response, Emma rubbed her tummy and licked her lips.

"I'll toss another in the pan," Sam said.

Dorthea fixed her attention on Emma. "Well, hello, darling."

"Hello!" Emma said.

"I love your yellow dress, sweetie." Dorthea laughed. "You have the prettiest dresses. Would you like some tea?"

"I'd prefer a soda," Emma said to Maria, but Lizzie caught her eye and shook her head.

"Milk or water."

Emma groaned and flopped down on the table as though she was dying. When that didn't work, she sat up, folded her hands and said, "Milk, please," for which she earned a motherly nod.

They'd just finished lunch when Crystal and Jack arrived. He was a few years older than Emma, and a boy, which was a concern for Lizzie at first—boys could be rough and tumble—but as she, Danny and Crystal sat on the porch and chatted while the kids played, she could tell Jack was a sweet, shy kid. Beyond that, Crystal had made it a point to pull out a pack of wipes and sanitize both their hands before Jack and Emma met.

When she commented on how well the two were

getting along, and Crystal said, "Well, I told him to be careful, on account of the fact that Emma's been sick," Lizzie knew immediately that she and Crystal were going to become fast friends. It would be nice to have someone in town to talk to, especially another mom.

"She's so much better now," Danny said.

Lizzie smiled at Crystal. "Still, I appreciate your thoughtfulness." To which Crystal flushed.

Sam, Mark and DJ came out to chat, too, but as soon as Luke saw who was on the porch, he made a one-eighty back into the house. Lizzie couldn't help noticing the flush that rose on his cheeks when the pretty waitress said, "Hi, Luke." She also noticed that Crystal's expression dropped when he didn't respond.

Maria brought out some lemonade for everyone, then took a glass to Dorthea, who had opted to stay inside the air-conditioned house. "This is so pleasant," Lizzie said, leaning against Danny as she sipped her drink.

"It is nice," he murmured.

"Just watching Emma play with another child... Oh. Oh. Rats. I forgot the sunscreen." Lizzie riffled through her purse and pulled out the tube. "Emma, come here, honey."

Danny chuckled. "She hasn't been out that long."

"Had I thought my worrying days are over?" she said on a laugh. Now there were just new things to worry about.

Emma endured the subsequent slathering—even though she clearly wanted to go join Jack on the swing set Luke had built. The moment Lizzie released her, she was off again.

Sam laughed. "Look at her go."

"Yes," Lizzie said. "Look at her go." It was a glorious sight.

Once the kids were worn out, they curled up in the family room to watch a video while the adults continued to chat in the parlor. Crystal had a great sense of humor and she was a wealth of knowledge on what entertained the kids in Butterscotch Ridge and hereabouts.

They invited Crystal and her son to stay for supper, but they had to decline because she had to work. It was hard for Lizzie to see her go.

"I like her," Danny said when they headed inside after seeing them off.

"Me, too," Lizzie said with a smile.

"Me three," Emma crowed.

"What did you think of Jack?" she asked as they made their way into the parlor where Maria had put out afternoon tea for Dorthea…and Emma.

"Nice. You know he goes to horse camp?"

"Does he?"

Her lip—*that* lip—came out. "I want to go to horse camp."

"What is horse camp, exactly?" Lizzie asked.

Danny shrugged. "No idea."

Sam chuckled. "It's where little kids learn how to ride horses."

"Safely," Luke added with a knowing look at Lizzie.

Emma nodded as she helped herself to one of the cookies in the arrangement. "Yes. That. That's what I want."

Danny and Lizzie exchanged a horrified glance, for which Lizzie was grateful. Clearly, he felt it was too soon to put Emma on a horse, as well. Thank heaven. Oh, if they stayed here, she would need to learn to ride. Of course she would. Just not yet.

"We just need to take it slow, pumpkin," Danny said. "Maybe when you're a little older?"

"How much older?"

"Ah…" His glance at Lizzie was a little panicked. Clearly, he didn't have a clue. Fortunately for him, just then, Maria poked her head into the room.

"Excuse me, Danny?"

He turned to face her. "Yes, Maria?"

"There's someone here to see you."

The relief on his face was comical so Lizzie murmured, "Saved by the bell," and they both chuckled. Emma's demand would have to wait.

"It's a woman," Maria added.

A woman? Lizzie met Danny's gaze in confusion.

Maria cleared her throat. "She says she's your *mother.*"

In that second, the world stopped turning.

Lizzie's lungs locked. Her pulse thudded hard. A slew of bitter memories sluiced through her.

Oh. Oh, *no*.

Her gaze snapped to Danny's face and she shuddered. His muscles were tight, his expression grim. He swallowed heavily, several times.

Everyone else froze, too, as though they felt the sudden tension crackling in the room. Silence hummed.

Danny's mother was *here*?

Lizzie's first instinct was to grab Emma, get in her car and drive back to Seattle as fast as possible.

This was a woman she'd vowed would never step foot into Emma's life. Not after everything she'd done to her son. Based on Danny's expression, and the tic in his cheek as he looked at Emma, he felt the same. Her heart pounded in sympathy. They both knew they needed to protect Emma from the ugly confrontation that was about to happen.

He nodded to her and she grabbed Emma's hand. "Come on, honey. Let's go to our room. I'll read you that book you love, the one about the runaway bunny."

Her daughter resisted. "What? Why? I want to meet Daddy's mom." With sudden strength, she yanked her little hand from Lizzie's and, before any of them could react, Emma ran from the room and into the foyer.

Lizzie leaped from the sofa to rush after her, but even then, it felt as though she was moving in slow motion. With Danny at her heels, they sprinted to the hall, coming to a stop as they took in a most horrific scene.

There she stood, all dressed in black, like a movie villainess, wearing more makeup than half the women in Butterscotch Ridge, and indifferently flicking ashes from her lit cigarette onto the hardwood floor. She stared down at the little girl who had run to greet her but who was now warily taking stock.

"Who are you?" Danny's mother drawled at Emma. Then she flicked her ash again.

"I'm Emma." She cocked her head. "You don't look like a grandma." She wrinkled her nose. "You don't smell like one, either."

She threw back her head then, the Gorgon of old with her basilisk stare, and sneered. "I should hope not."

"My other grandma is *cozy*."

"Emma. Sweetie." Lizzie eased closer, carefully, cautiously, like a mother trying to distract a tiger from her baby. But Danny got to her first, and scooped up Emma in a rush. He understood far too well that this woman was a danger. To all of them.

"Ah." Her blood-red lips curled. She simpered as she surveyed her son holding his child protectively in his arms. "Perhaps I am a grandmother after all."

Danny stared at his mother in shock and horror. She was here. She'd found him.

Had he really thought he was done with her forever? Was he still so naive?

DJ, Mark, Luke and Sam stumbled to a halt in the foyer and gaped at her, as well. Must have been quite the tableau, with all eyes on *her*. As she demanded.

Oh, she was still as beautiful as ever, but in a hardened kind of way. There might have been some Botox since Danny had last seen her. Regardless, she seemed as intractable as ever.

DJ stepped forward, waving his siblings back behind him. Which was wise. Snakes could strike without any warning. "Excuse me. Who are you?" he asked.

Her gaze found him. "Why, I'm Daniel's mother," she said, holding out her hand. As though she wanted him to kiss it or something. "I'm *Patrice*." She always said her name that way, as though it was something people *should* recognize.

"You're a redhead," Danny said. First thought that bubbled up through the morass of emotions.

His mother fingered her coif with her sharp, glossy nails. "Do you like it?" She took another puff. "I think it suits me. It did get blown to hell, though. Teach me to drive a convertible in the desert."

Danny glanced out the window at the flashy sports car in the drive and sighed. "Where'd you get the car, Mother?"

Her expression soured. "I don't have to explain myself to you."

"Fine." His tone was stoic. It had to be. If he let any emotion show, he might not be able to rein it back in again. "Why are you here?"

"Don't you know?" She fluttered her long lashes. "I came to pay my respects." She turned to the rest of the family and Maria, who were watching this circus with dumbstruck expressions. "I am so sorry for your loss." She uttered these words as though she'd rehearsed all the way here.

A muscle jerked in Danny's cheek, but he tried to keep his expression impassive. He nodded at his mother. "All right then. You've done that. Now you can leave."

"Leave?" She stepped closer. Danny passed Emma to Lizzie and moved in front of them. "Why on earth would I leave? I just arrived. I want to spend some time with my beloved son." Her gaze flicked to Emma, then back to Danny, and her lips quirked. "And my granddaughter. Aren't you glad to see me?"

Apparently, his expression made his opinion clear.

Patrice sighed and ground out her cigarette with the toe of her Louboutin. "Christ. I just drove a thousand miles to see you. Aren't you even going to offer me something to drink?"

"Of course," DJ said, and Danny's head whipped

around so he could gape at his brother in disbelief.
"What would you like?"

Patrice smiled at him, a little too seductively for
Danny's comfort. "Well, aren't you the country gen-
tleman? I'll take a whiskey. Neat." Then his mother
lifted a long, dancer's leg and massaged her calf, all
while holding DJ's gaze. "It was a very long drive.
Do you mind if I sit?"

For some reason, DJ smiled. "Sure. Why don't
we all head to my office and chat there? It's more...
intimate."

Danny looked at Lizzie, who appeared as dumbfounded as he felt. Could his brother not see what
they were dealing with? Or was his mother so slick
that anyone who didn't know her could be fooled?
He hated that thought. DJ was a good and decent
person. All of them were. They deserved better than
to be conned by Patrice Diem.

But then DJ turned to Emma, offered her a broad
grin and said, "Hey, sweetie. Why don't you help
Maria make some cookies for later?" With that,
Danny's fears began to melt away. He realized his
brother's intent was to cut Emma from the herd, to
protect her from danger. He had the sudden urge
to hug him.

Emma pouted. "But I want to watch."

Lizzie kissed the curls sprouting on her daughter's head. "Oh, your daddy just needs to talk to
his mom about boring grown-up stuff because they
haven't seen each other in a while. We'll tell you

all about it later. Okay? So go ahead with Maria, like DJ said, okay?"

"I am making peanut-butter-sandwich cookies," Maria said with a wink.

Emma wriggled out of Lizzie's arms. "With blackberry jam?"

Maria made a shocked face. "Is there any other kind?" She held out her hand to Emma and led the little girl into the kitchen, whispering about all the cookies they would get to eat by themselves while the others were distracted.

Danny felt Lizzie lean into him with relief. Thank God, DJ had been able to distract their daughter from this mess. Because with his mother, it was just going to get messier. It always did.

DJ led the way to his office, but he subtly blocked his siblings from entering after Danny and his mother. He tried to exclude Lizzie, too, but she gave him *the look* and pushed past him into the office. Lizzie took a seat behind the giant desk with her arms crossed, indicating she was here for one reason only, and that was to be present for him. Her expression said clearly, *I'm here for you.*

It gave him strength, having her behind him. Having all of them. He knew this was his battle to fight, but it was damn nice that he wasn't alone in it.

His mother took a moment to assess the office, the stately river rock fireplace, weathered beams, bright open windows that let the sunlight in, the mahogany desk, still covered with paperwork Lizzie had been working on this morning. As Danny and DJ rearranged the chairs by the fireplace, she paused by the credenza to heft the bronze statue of Zeus, as though estimating its value. Danny had the urge to rip it from her fingers before she could stuff it into her purse.

"Please, sit." How DJ managed to maintain his hospitable tone was a mystery.

"And my drink?" Patrice set her hand on her hip, as though to say, *not moving 'til I get it*.

In response, DJ opened the credenza, pulled out a whiskey bottle and a crystal glass and poured Patrice a few fingers. She knocked them back like water and held out the glass for more. "Shall we sit?" he said again, after he refilled her glass. Danny noticed he kept hold of the bottle, so maybe he wasn't as gullible as he seemed.

"So," DJ said, almost like a mediator, once the three of them were settled in a semicircle. "Tell us why you're here."

Patrice smiled at him. "That should be obvious. I came to see my boy." She touched Danny's hand.

He jerked out of reach.

She reacted to this rebuff with a softening of her expression, her stance, her tear ducts. A melodramatic sniffle. He knew better.

"Why are you really here?" he asked.

His mother fished through her bag for a tissue and then delicately sobbed into it. "I've come all this way to see you. I've missed you." She looked up at him, her beautiful eyes wide and damp. "You're my only son. My baby. I love you."

Danny stared at her, the well of his patience for her cold and empty. He knew her. He knew her ploys. She'd always counted on her emotional hold on Danny to manipulate him. And he'd always fallen for it, too desperate for whatever short-lived affection she might deign to show him. Not this time.

Now, he knew what real love was. He wouldn't be fooled by the fake stuff ever again.

"Are you still running from the law?" he asked blandly.

Her expression tightened. "Seriously?" The soft, sweet, vulnerable tone melted into a bitter snarl. "You're going to bring that up?"

Danny shook his head. "Mother, you skipped bail."

She shrugged. "I needed to get out of town."

"You know I posted your bail, right?"

"And I never got a chance to say thank you."

"You knew I didn't have that kind of money. You knew I had to borrow it."

Her lips pursed. "I *said* thank you."

Technically, she hadn't.

"I had to borrow that money from Mikey Gerardo."

Her eyes widened. "You borrowed money from Mikey Gerardo?"

"Yes, Mother. I did."

She barked a harsh laugh. "Well, that was stupid."

Danny was silent for a moment as fury and frustration raked him. "Really?" he finally said. "Was it a stupid thing? My mother was in jail. How else could I come up with the bail money?"

"But a loan shark?" The smirk on Patrice's painted face was infuriating. "Really, Danny?"

"Right. I should have just gone to the bank and asked for five grand to bail my mother out. With no assets. How do you think that would have gone?"

"You could have just left me there. In jail."

"Maybe I should have."

Patrice dug through her bag for a cigarette and lit up. "Well, that's all behind us now, isn't it? Now that you've been named in your grandfather's will?" She took hold of Danny's arm. He tried to disengage, but couldn't. Patrice tightened her hold, leaned in and hissed in what could have been considered a doting tone, if one didn't know her, "My son. The *heir*."

Lizzie's gut lurched. Rage nearly blinded her. It took everything in her to stay silent, to let Danny work through this on his own. She had the suspicion he needed this confrontation, this confirmation of the fact that he was nothing like his mother.

"So this is about money?" he asked. He sounded tired.

Patrice arched an eyebrow. "I would think you could spare some now."

"Mother, I don't have any money. I work here at the ranch for wages—just like everybody else." His tone was tight.

She tossed back her head. "I find that hard to believe."

DJ cleared his throat. "That is, in fact, how we operate, ma'am," he said in a deeper voice than usual. "Our profit goes right back into the herd. Why, veterinary costs alone—"

"So sell a cow. Or a tractor. Or whatever. I don't care, as long as I get my money."

"*Your* money?" Danny gaped at her.

Patrice's gaze narrowed on him. "You owe me."

He snorted harshly. "I owe *you*? For what?"

"I raised you. I sacrificed for you. Do you have any idea how many men want nothing to do with a woman who has a child? Do you know how many opportunities I had to pass up because I had a snot-nosed brat at home?"

Lizzie's gut roiled at every word. How dare she try to make Danny feel guilty? She'd been the worst mother on the face of the earth. People like Patrice Diem should never be allowed to have children. It was—

Her breath locked as a suspicion blossomed, then certainty. She quickly flipped through the folders she'd been working on this morning and found the one she was looking for. The one that outlined those mysterious payments they hadn't been able to identify. The ones that had been made for the whole of

Danny's life. "Oh, my God," she said to DJ, holding up the folder. "She's PD!"

DJ's eyes narrowed. He turned his dark gaze on Patrice. "Of course. That makes perfect sense."

It explained so much. Why Patrice always seemed to have everything she wanted—chic clothes, salon visits and money to party all the time while Danny had had to scavenge for food as a child. This woman had taken that money from Danny's father for years. And she'd spent every penny on herself.

"What makes perfect sense?" Danny asked. "What are you two talking about?"

DJ nodded to Lizzie. "You tell him."

She leaped to her feet and carried the evidence to him. "We were curious about this file earlier. Years and years of payments we couldn't account for. Your father *did* send money to you. For years. And after your dad died, your grandfather continued sending the money regularly."

Danny flipped through the incriminating pages, his expression growing more stunned by the moment.

"Isn't it true that you received regular support payments from us?" DJ demanded.

Patrice sputtered for a moment and then shook her head in an act of innocence they all saw through. "How could I remember something like that?"

Danny's expression tightened as he realized the agonizing truth of these documents. A mottled flush rose on his neck. "Oh, my God." He clapped his hand to his forehead. Raked his fingers through his hair. "How did I not see this coming? You lied to me my entire life. I should have realized you'd lied about this, too. You told me my father didn't give a damn. You said he didn't want anything to do with me." He pounded his chest. "You made me hate him. He was my father and you made me hate him. You made me think I wasn't worthy of his love. You lied to me about everything."

Patrice tipped her nose and sniffed. "Not everything."

"So you didn't lie when you told me my father didn't give a damn about me?"

"Oh, quit being so melodramatic."

"Melodramatic? Melodramatic? You emptied my bank accounts, pawned everything I own, skipped out on bail money I'd put my life on the line to secure—"

"I knew you'd land on your feet. You always do."

Thank the Lord, DJ interrupted, because Lizzie was about to lose it. She stood behind Danny, with her hand on his shoulder, and hopefully wasn't gouging him with her fingernails as she struggled to hold back.

"It seems to me," DJ said coolly, "if anyone owes someone money here, Patrice, *you* owe *Danny*."

Her nostrils flared. She leaped to her feet. "What nonsense."

"Ten thousand dollars. For bail." His smile was

like slate. Hard and cold and stony. "We don't take checks."

Patrice paled. Her throat worked. "My bail was only five."

DJ nodded. "You know loan sharks charge exorbitant interest, right? You do understand that."

"Oh, this is all beside the point." She began to pace, perhaps looking for an escape. "Obviously, you have plenty of money lying around. I don't see why you can't give me *something*."

"We don't just hand out money on this ranch." DJ stroked his chin. "You could work for it, though," he said ingenuously. "We could always use help mucking out stalls."

Patrice's eyes widened in horror; a red flush rose on her face. She whirled on Danny. "Are you going to let him treat me like this?"

Danny shrugged. "Pretty much. And I think you should go. Now," he said, his tone steely.

"But Danny..." A woeful plea.

"Sorry, Mother. I'm done. Done."

"Done? What do you mean 'done'?" She honestly seemed baffled. "I'm your mother."

He stared at her. "You gave birth to me, but I spent most of my life trying to figure out what I did to make you hate me so much. Or trying to figure out what I could do to make you love me. Eventually I realized it didn't matter what *I* did, because you would only care about yourself.

"I came here not expecting much of anything.

Definitely not expecting to find out that I had a family here. A real family. They accepted me. They welcomed me. They gave me a place to live. A job. They gave me a chance to prove myself, to make a place for myself here." He hesitated, swallowed. "And when my child needed help, they moved heaven and earth to do so. Even though we were still all new to each other. So I know now who my real family is. Who I can count on. And I'm sorry, Mother, but it doesn't look like that's ever been you."

She stared at him for a long while, calculating. Perhaps she realized, finally, that her emotional ploys would no longer work, because she took a deep cleansing breath and said, "I can see you're upset. Maybe I should come back at another time."

He shook his head. "It won't make any difference. My feelings aren't going to change."

She dropped her cigarette in the crystal glass, then collected her things. "Of course they will. Listen, I'm staying at the Butterscotch Inn. When you feel better, call me. Okay?"

"You're staying here? In town?" Lizzie blurted out.

Patrice tucked her hair behind her ear and smiled. "Yes. Peter and I have a room."

"Peter?" DJ asked.

Patrice batted her lashes at him. "He's just a friend."

Right.

DJ was hardly swayed. "Well, I gotta say, I agree with Danny. It might be a good idea if you left now. Seeing as the local sheriff is my poker buddy, it's pretty likely I might mention your presence here next time we get together. As you're a wanted woman and all."

Danny could tell his mother got the point. Her expression tightened. Her smile grew even more brittle. She gathered her things and cleared her throat. "Well, this has been pleasant, but I really must be off now. Much obliged for the drink."

As she sashayed from the room, clutching her purse with both hands, DJ was there to open the door for her. Lizzie and Danny followed, just to make sure she left. It was a relief to watch her head out the door, down the steps and to her car. *Someone's* car.

They all followed and stood on the porch and watched as Patrice lit another cigarette, gunned the engine and left in a spray of gravel.

Chapter Thirteen

Danny stood silently, staring at the cloud in his mother's wake.

"Are you okay?" Lizzie asked.

"Yeah," he said. But in truth, he reeled. This was all so much to take in. The good. The bad. The really ugly.

At the same time, he felt free in a way he never had before. His father hadn't rejected him. That in itself was huge.

His father *had* wanted him. He had. His mother had kept them apart simply so the money would keep coming.

He took Lizzie's hand and they headed, together, to the kitchen, to Emma. He scooped his daughter up in his arms—cookie-batter-covered spatula and all—and held her tight.

He willed his heart to cease its pounding, gasped to try to normalize his breath as gratitude and fury warred within him.

Oh, he'd faced his mother in her rages more times than he could count. He'd suffered her abuse—which now, as an adult, he recognized as mental, physical and emotional. His whole life, he'd struggled to protect himself from the damage that followed in her wake.

But he'd never been as frightened as he had been the moment his mother's gaze landed on Emma. He'd recognized that predatory *look* in her eye. He would do anything to protect Emma from Patrice Diem. No matter what.

"Daddy? Daddy! You're squeezing me tight."

"Oh, I'm sorry, hon." He relaxed his hold. A little. "It's just that I love you so much."

She leaned back and smeared at the wetness on his cheeks with her palms. "Why are you crying?"

He sniffed. "I'm not crying."

"Yes, you are."

"Hey. What is that? Peanut-butter cookie dough?" He peered into the bowl.

She laughed. "We finished those. These are chocolate chip."

He leaned in and nibbled at the spatula. "My favorite."

Emma made a cute little-girl face, pulled away

the spatula and told him sternly, "You're not supposed to eat it raw."

"I know. But it's good." He grinned at her as he stood and released her.

Emma glanced around the kitchen. "Where's that other grandma lady?"

Danny dropped down into one of the kitchen chairs and pulled her onto his lap. "She had to leave, honey."

Emma wrinkled her face. "Why did she have to leave? Isn't she your mom?"

He glanced at Lizzie, a plea for help, perhaps. This conversation was a little beyond him right now.

Of course, she stepped right in. "She just stopped by on her way through town. Wow. Those cookies look good. Can I have a nibble?"

But kids weren't stupid. Emma knew something had upset Danny. She patted his cheek, then became fascinated with the rub of his day beard. "I love you, Daddy," she said. "Please don't be sad."

Such simple words.

They broke his heart and filled it, all at the same time. He pulled her closer. "I love you, too, Emma. More than I can ever tell you. I want you to know that, no matter what, I love you and I always will."

"Even if I'm naughty?"

He smiled and kissed the top of her head. "Even if you're naughty."

Lizzie sighed. "But maybe try not to be naughty," she suggested and everyone laughed.

Danny looked around the kitchen at all the smiling faces, and something swelled in his chest.

It was beautiful, wasn't it?

Family?

The real kind?

All that mattered, really, ever, was love.

It was damn nice to have it.

After that scene with his mother, after all the revelations, Danny needed to get out of the house, so he asked Lizzie if she wanted to go for a walk to the pond, and she agreed.

"How are you doing?" she asked as they set out.

He shrugged. "Getting there."

"Pretty tough, having her show up like that."

Danny sighed. "My mother is, and always has been, selfish as hell. When I was a child, I thought it was me. My fault. Like maybe there was something wrong with me to make her not love me." As much as it hurt him to think these things, relive them, say them, it felt right to finally tell Lizzie what had been slithering around inside him all this time. It felt good to bring it to light. It felt as though the weight he'd been carrying for years was sloughing off and falling to the dirt.

She squeezed his hand. "There's nothing wrong with you."

He tried not to laugh, but succeeded only in compressing it into a snort. "No. After a while, I realized it was just her. She wouldn't have loved any kid she had. She learned how to be a mother from her mom. Her mom was pretty mean, too. It kind of makes me sad for her, because no one ever showed her what it's like to really love someone."

Lizzie cuddled closer. "That is sad."

"I agree." He turned to her. "I want something better for us. And Emma."

She studied him a moment, then smiled. "You've changed, Danny Diem. You know that, don't you?"

He huffed a breath. "I've had to take a long hard look at myself. At who I was, and who I could be, and who I wanted to be. Especially since I…found you again. And Emma."

"That's a lot to think about."

"Yeah. I realized that we have control. We don't have to follow the path our parents set us on if we don't want to. We can change who we are. I didn't like the man I'd become, hard and resentful, but I had a choice. I could stay the same, or I could let go of all that anger and bitterness and make my life what I wanted it to be." He gazed into her eyes and smiled. "We can't choose our parents, but we can choose our families. And I choose you. Both of you."

For some reason, tears welled in Lizzie's beautiful eyes. Maybe he shouldn't have gotten so sappy.

"I admit, at first I was scared to death about being a parent. I guess everyone is. But now? Now, Lizzie, I can't tell you how thankful I am that you gave me a chance to try."

"You're her father."

"Her sperm donor," he said on a laugh.

"No." Her voice was stern. "You're her father and you know it."

They walked for a bit more, enjoying the cool breezes of the coming summer evening and the rustling in the trees. He squeezed her shoulder. "How are you doing?" he asked.

The look she sent him was wry and knowing. "Why don't you ask me what you really want to ask, Danny?"

Damn. She knew him pretty well. He squared his shoulders and cleared his throat. "Are you happy here? At the ranch?"

She nodded. "Yes. I love it here."

"And would you and Emma consider staying?" He said it so softly that he was afraid she missed it.

But she didn't. She cupped his cheek and stared into his eyes. "Yes."

It took a second for her meaning to percolate through his brain, what that *yes* meant—that he finally had what he wanted, what he'd always wanted, and how damn happy that made him. With a jubilant whoop, he grabbed her up and twirled her around.

It wasn't until later that night—after Emma had been put to bed and Lizzie and Danny had made love and she'd fallen asleep—that Mark's question from long ago surfaced in Danny's brain.

Are you going to marry her?

Danny's first and immediate response at the time had been *no*. It was his default position on the subject and always had been. His entire life, *marriage* had been a dirty word. A heinous, precarious place where only pain and betrayal awaited.

But when he was with Lizzie, he didn't feel like that. Never had. When he was with Lizzie, he was happy. Happy, as he never had been before.

So why did the thought of marrying her—or anyone—turn his stomach?

Marriage was forever. He wanted Lizzie forever.

Marriage meant a partnership. They already had that.

What else was it? Why was it so scary?

He already loved her—more than he could bear—so there was no risk in making everything official. So why…?

And then it hit him. It hit him—in a wash of pent-up fears and seeping wounds from the past.

The reason he shied away from marriage was because, in some deep, dark corner of his soul, he believed he, himself, was not worthy of being loved. That surely, one day, she would realize the truth, see his flaws and desert him. Forever. He'd be alone.

He stared down at her as she slept, sweet and beautiful and good-hearted. And he smiled because now that he'd faced it, that fear was utterly gone.

The first thing the next morning, Danny sought out his daughter. Sure, he'd made a momentous decision in the night, but before he could do anything, he had to talk to Emma.

He found her by the rabbit hutch Luke had built her, staring at the bunnies.

"Hi, Daddy." She waved.

"Hey, sweetie. Can I tear you away from the bunnies for a minute? I have something very important to talk to you about."

She wrinkled her nose. "Is this about going back to the hospital?"

He kneeled beside her and met her gaze. "No. No, it's not."

"Because I like it here and I don't want to go back."

"It's not about that. I promise."

"Okay."

They walked together to a nearby bench at the garden entrance and sat. "This is serious," he said, just so she knew he meant business.

"Okay."

"Emma, you know how much I love your mommy." His heart thudded. "And you know how much I love you."

Her nod was minuscule.

"And I would very much like to ask your mom to marry me. But—"

"But?"

He swallowed. Hard. "Well, you're the most important person in her life. I wanted to ask you for your permission first. You know, make sure you're okay with having a real forever daddy." He glanced at her hopefully.

She raised an eyebrow. Surveyed him silently for a long moment. His skin prickled. Something trickled down his spine. Then she tipped up her dimpled chin and asked, "If you marry Mommy, will I get a pony?"

He gaped at her. "What?"

"Can I have a pony?"

Words failed him. He sputtered for a moment, then asked, "Are you blackmailing me?"

She looked confused. "I don't know what that is."

Duh, cowboy, he thought. *Now go and explain that one*. "It's when you try to force someone to get you a pony."

"Oh." She thought on this for a moment. "Well, I do think you are an awesome daddy…"

"Thank you."

"And Mommy seems to like you." Thank God for that. "If we get married, can we all stay together? Forever?"

He loved that she said *we*. "Yes. We would definitely stay together."

She thought about it for a moment, tapping her lip. And then she smiled. "Yeah. I guess it's okay." And then, as he hugged her, she added, "But I'd still like a pony. Or a goat."

When Lizzie emerged from the office for dinner that night, the table was only set for six. She smiled when Sam and Emma came in with the glasses; Sam supervised as Emma set them above the spoons. "Who's not coming?" she asked. To which Emma grinned and Sam batted her lashes as though she had something in her eye.

"You!" Emma said, and then dissolved into chortles.

Sam nudged her with an elbow. "Shh. It's a surprise."

Lizzie set her hands on her hips and narrowed her eyes at Emma. She didn't know Sam all that well, but she knew her daughter couldn't keep a secret if her life depended on it. The fact that Emma then folded her hands and tried to look innocent clinched it.

"Ahem."

She whirled at the deep, familiar voice. Danny stood in the arched entry looking... Wow. He was wearing a suit. And, damn, he looked good. Her pulse heated. "What...?" It was all she could manage.

He stepped forward and took her hand. "We're going on a date tonight."

Her heart did a little flip-flop. "A date?"

"In the rose garden!" Emma called out, then covered her mouth with her hands. More chortles ensued.

"Ooh. In the rose garden?" Lizzie couldn't stop her smile. Probably because his was infectious. "But I'm not dressed for a fancy date."

He pulled her closer and took her in his arms. Kissed her forehead. "You look perfect. Shall we?"

"All right," she said, taking his proffered arm and following him into the kitchen. Sam and Emma trailed behind them. To Lizzie's surprise, everyone was in the kitchen. DJ, Mark, Luke, Maria, even Dorthea. And they all grinned as though they knew a secret. But as she and Danny continued on to the patio, no one followed. Thank God.

It was a beautiful summer evening. She sighed as Danny led her into the garden, to a table that had been set under the pergola entwined with flowers and wrapped with pretty white lights. The table was set exquisitely, with crystal glasses, linens and everything. A champagne bottle chilled in a bucket.

"Danny?"

"Hush." He gave her a kiss and then pulled out her chair. "Milady?"

She had to giggle. Lordy. She hadn't *giggled* in decades. "Danny, what is this?"

He shrugged. "I thought we deserved a romantic dinner. You know. A chance to talk. Privately?"

"Oh, yes. That's a lovely idea." She reached across the table and took his hand.

"And…" He cleared his throat. "I wanted to thank you."

Lizzie blinked. "Thank me?"

"Yes." His eyes glowed a little. But those couldn't be tears. Could they? "I'm so happy you're back in my life. That we're together. And so freaking grateful that you brought me Emma. I love her so much—"

Awesome. Now she was tearing up, too. His expression was filled with so much gratitude, it humbled her. "She loves you, as well." She squeezed his hand.

"But it's more than that. I'm…changed. A changed man. In so many ways."

She nodded. She could tell.

"So much of that is because you and Emma are in my life."

"So much of that is because you chose to deal with your past." She could see it in his face, his smile, his eyes. The bitterness was gone. The haunted looks, erased. The uncertainty about his place in the world, evaporated. "I am so proud of you."

Her words hit him hard for some reason. He opened his mouth but no words came out. So instead, he lifted her hand and kissed it, reverently. "Lizzie. I—"

"Dinner!"

Lizzie jumped at the warbled cry. Emma appeared with Maria in her wake, carrying a tray. Emma proudly set the bread basket on the table as Maria set earthenware bowls before them. Maria then melted away, but Emma remained, watching them both with a zeal she usually reserved for *Dora the Explorer*.

Lizzie glanced down at the crusted bowl. "So... what are we having?"

"Chicken pot pie," Danny said with a wink. "Emma told me it's your favorite."

She nearly snorted a laugh. Lobster was her favorite. Emma was the one who loved chicken pot pie. "It smells wonderful."

"I helped Daddy make it," Emma said.

Lizzie lifted an eyebrow at Danny. "*You* made this?" How sweet.

"I had help."

"Thank you."

Lizzie cracked the crust. Steam erupted. A delicious aroma swelled before her.

She took a tentative bite. Oh. It was delicious. But...she had to spit it out, a decidedly unromantic thing to do, because there was something hard in the—

Oh, good glory.

She stared at her spoon, where something glittered. It was...a ring. A pretty sapphire ring. Sapphires were her birthstone.

As the significance of this hit her, her pulse fluttered. Her head went light. Her gaze snapped to Danny's face. His Adam's apple bobbed.

He'd sworn he would never marry. He'd said it a hundred times. A thousand. What on earth was this?

Oh, but she knew. His expression made her chest ache. So sweet. So sincere. So...scared.

He ran a finger around his collar and cleared

his throat. "Since the moment I met you, I knew you were special. And all these years later, you still make my heart pound when you're near. And now…" He gestured to Emma. "I couldn't be happier with us as a family. I…" He swallowed again, then looked her in the eye. "I love you, Elizabeth Michaels. More than I ever thought was possible. In fact, I—"

"Oh, come on. Can we get this over with?" The smallest person at the table had the shortest attention span. "I want a forever family and I'm hungry. Just say yes already, Mommy."

Lizzie frowned at her daughter. "Shouldn't I tell him how much I love him, too, before I say yes?"

Emma rolled her eyes. "Oh, all right."

"Well," she said, her chest tight, her emotions in a flurry. "I love you, Danny Diem. I love your strength, your heart. I love your willingness to adapt and change. I love the way you embraced… both of us—"

Emma sighed.

"Of course, I will marry you, Danny."

"Woo-hoo! She said yes!" Emma bellowed, apparently to the family, because the kitchen door opened and everyone flooded into the garden, crowing and cheering and—in Sam's case—tossing confetti. But all this hullabaloo was lost on Lizzie, who was staring into the eyes of the man she loved, the man she would spend the rest of her life with.

The man who wanted to marry her.

Marry. Her.

It was hard to keep from smiling, even as he kissed her.

Everyone was so excited about celebrating the successful proposal that bedtime came late that night. Sam and Emma sat around forever talking about wedding stuff. Emma was pretty sure there should be ponies.

When Lizzie glanced at the clock, she was surprised at how quickly the evening had passed. "Oh, my goodness. Emma Jean. It's way late. Time for you to go to bed."

Naturally, Emma protested, but Lizzie could see she was tired. So she told her that tomorrow they could go into town and look over the church to see if it would be a good place for the wedding, even though Dorthea wanted to do it right here, in the garden.

As for Danny, he didn't care where they held the wedding. He just wanted to marry Lizzie. Wherever. Whenever. However.

He also longed to get his fiancée alone, even though there was no rush. They had time. They had all the time in the world.

Fortunately, despite her protests, Emma fell asleep before they got halfway through her bedtime story. He and Lizzie rose together and, hand in hand, headed to his room. Once there, she wrapped her arms around his neck and pulled him close.

Not for a kiss, though.

"You realize you proposed to me over chicken pot pie?" she said.

He grinned. "I didn't want to be pretentious."

"Well, it worked." She snorted. "The unpretentious part."

He kissed her soundly. "I am so happy you agreed to marry me. Knowing everything about me. You still want me."

She rubbed his nose with hers. "I still want you. Imagine that."

He smiled, but it was a little wobbly. Something prickled in his eye. "I don't know what I ever did to deserve you—"

She made a face. "I hate that word. I'm just glad you chose to be the man you are, Daniel Diem, because I love who you are." She kissed him then, softly, the way he liked it.

Then she pushed him back onto the bed and straddled him. He liked that better.

"You decided," she said. "You made the choice to be your own man, and I'm so glad of it."

"I am, too," he said.

She slid off him—*damn*—and cuddled at his side with her ring hand on his chest. The stone caught the light and flashed. "You chose us. Me. And Emma..." She trailed off in a way that made something shimmy up his spine.

He strummed his thumb on her arm. "Of course I chose you."

She leaned up on her elbow and looked down at him. Her face was nearly obscured by her hair, but he could see her eyes. "And all that nonsense about you not being a good father is over, right? Because you are a good father. You're a great father. You're gentle and caring and you make sacrifices for Emma, which is what real parents do." She cupped his face. "You are the best father ever." Her lips were warm on his, but it was nothing to the warmth rising in his chest.

He *had* chosen.

He'd chosen to let go of his fears and step fully into the role fate had given him. And it was a wonderful role. The best. Emma's dad.

He deepened the kiss and pulled Lizzie against him before rolling over so he was on top. He growled a little and rubbed against her, and she laughed. "I chose you," he said before kissing her nose. Her eyelid. Her earlobe. Her lips.

She opened to him like a flower. But he pulled away. He wasn't done yet. This was important stuff.

"I chose Emma, too."

She set her palm on his cheek. "You did. And any children yet to come."

He stilled. His heart thudded. "Yet to come?" He hadn't even thought that far ahead. Oh, how amazing would it be to have a herd of them? Rough-and-tumble little boys and bunny-loving little girls?

Lizzie punched his shoulder. Apparently to get

his attention back. "Hey. What's wrong? Don't you want more children?" Her adorable brow furrowed.

"I most certainly do," he said, and then he sealed it with a kiss. It was a very romantic kiss. He had no idea why she pushed him back right in the middle of it.

"Good," she said. She said it with a very particular look in her eye. One that meant…

His breath caught in his throat. A hum rose in his ears. His heart hiccupped. "Oh, my God!" He gaped at her. "Are you…? Is it…? Did we…?"

She laughed. "Yes. To all of those questions."

He kissed her soundly. "When? What? How?"

She made a face. "I think you know how." But then she smiled. Why wouldn't she? "I'm three months along."

"Three months?" With reverence, he set his hand on her flat belly. In there. Somewhere in there… was his child. A little boy, or another little girl like Emma. "That means…"

"A baby for Christmas?" Her smile was just brilliant.

"A Christmas baby." Perfect.

Just perfect.

Everything was perfect.

And everything he'd been through in his life? It had brought him to this moment. This place. All the suffering and anguish had meant something because it had helped him become who he was. A man who had earned the love of a good woman. Who had earned a chance to be a great dad, who was finally happy in his own skin.

He pulled Lizzie close, kissed her on the forehead and whispered again how much he adored her.

She grunted, then caught his eye and muttered, "Chicken pot pie? Seriously?"

And they both had to laugh, each knowing that they had found their place. Together. Forever.

* * * * *

Look for Mark's story,
Recipe for a Homecoming,
the next book in New York Times *bestselling author
Sabrina York's The Stirling Ranch miniseries
on sale October 2021
wherever Harlequin Special Edition
books and ebooks are sold.*

WE HOPE YOU ENJOYED
THIS BOOK FROM

HARLEQUIN
SPECIAL
EDITION

Believe in love. Overcome obstacles. Find happiness.

Relate to finding comfort and strength in the
support of loved ones and enjoy the journey
no matter what life throws your way.

6 NEW BOOKS AVAILABLE EVERY MONTH!

HSEHALO2021

COMING NEXT MONTH FROM

H HARLEQUIN

SPECIAL EDITION

#2857 THE MOST ELIGIBLE COWBOY
Montana Mavericks: The Real Cowboys of Bronco Heights
by Melissa Senate

Brandon Taylor has zero interest in tying the knot—until his unexpected fling with ex-girlfriend Cassidy Ware. Now she's pregnant—but Cassidy is not jumping at his practical proposal. She remembers their high school romance all too well, and she won't wed without proof that Brandon 2.0 can be the *real* husband she longs for.

#2858 THE LATE BLOOMER'S ROAD TO LOVE
Matchmaking Mamas • by Marie Ferrarella

When other girls her age were dating and finding love, Rachel Fenelli was keeping the family restaurant going after her father's heart attack. Now she's on the verge of starting the life she should have started years ago. Enter Wyatt Watson, the only physical therapist her stubborn dad will tolerate. But little does Rachel know that her dad has an ulterior—matchmaking?—motive!

#2859 THE PUPPY PROBLEM
Paradise Pets • by Katie Meyer

There's nothing single mom Megan Palmer wouldn't do to help her son, Owen. So when his school tries to keep his autism service dog out of the classroom, Megan goes straight to the principal's office—and meets Luke Wright. He's impressed by her, and the more they work together, the more he hopes to win her over...

#2860 A DELICIOUS DILEMMA
by Sera Taíno

Val Navarro knew she shouldn't go dancing right after a bad breakup and she definitely shouldn't be thinking the handsome, sensitive stranger she meets could be more than a rebound. Especially after she finds out his father's company could shut down her Puerto Rican restaurant and unravel her tight-knit neighborhood. Is following her heart a recipe for disaster?

#2861 LAST-CHANCE MARRIAGE RESCUE
Top Dog Dude Ranch • by Catherine Mann

Nina and Douglas Archer are on the verge of divorce, but they're both determined to keep it together for one last family vacation, planned by their ten-year-old twins. And when they do, they're surprised to find themselves giving in to the romance of it all. Still, Nina knows she needs an emotionally available husband. Will a once-in-a-lifetime trip show them the way back to each other?

#2862 THE FAMILY SHE DIDN'T EXPECT
The Culhanes of Cedar River • by Helen Lacey

Marnie Jackson has one mission: to discover her roots in Cedar River. She's determined to fulfill her mother's dying wish, but her sexy landlord and his charming daughters turn out to be a surprising distraction from her goal. Widower Joss Culhane has been focusing on work, his kids and his own family drama. Why risk opening his heart to another woman who might leave them?

YOU CAN FIND MORE INFORMATION ON UPCOMING HARLEQUIN TITLES, FREE EXCERPTS AND MORE AT HARLEQUIN.COM.

HSECNM0821